GW00725522

Tales of Modern Stupidity

QUINTIN FORREST

First published in 2014

All Rights Reserved

© Quintin Forrest

The right of Quintin Forrest to be identified as author of
this work has been asserted in accordance with Section 77
of the Copyright, Designs and Patents Act of 1988

This book is sold subject to the condition that it shall not,
by way of trade or otherwise, be lent, resold, hired out, or
otherwise circulated without the author's prior consent in
any form of binding or cover other than that in which it is
published and without a similar condition, including this
condition, being imposed on the subsequent purchaser.

Printed by CreateSpace

ISBN 978-1-5008896-5-4

Cover design by Jon Cartwright and Dan Nyman

Cover image © Jon Cartwright 2013

Thanks to Katy, Jon and Dan.

CONTENTS

LAVENDER BUNNY AND THE BIG BROTHER HOUSE

'Can Lavender Bunny come to the Diary Room?'

'He says, no.'

'Michael, Big Brother is ordering Lavender Bunny to come to the Diary Room.'

'He says he doesn't like it in there. He says it smells of madness, and despair.'

'Michael, if Lavender Bunny does not come to the Diary Room immediately, he will be severely punished.'

'You better go, mate,' said one of the others. There were five of us out there, sunbathing on the lawn.

'Lavender Bunny says what are you going to do, put him up for eviction? He says that didn't work last time, did it? Or the time before that . . .'

'Michael, if Lavender Bunny does not come to the Diary Room immediately, Big Brother will have no choice but to take him into custody.'

'He says you'll have to prise him from my cold, dead hand.'

So what had driven us in there, me and LB? That was the question we'd keep coming back to.

Well, it was something to do with my debut novel, *Beer, Football And Shagging*. Finishing it up, I'd been thinking of ways of trying to improve my profile, before my agent sent it out. It was no use trusting to talent it seemed, or not to my talent anyway, at a time when Britain's most feted authors included Jordan, Wayne Rooney and Jeremy Clarkson. But I hadn't come up with much of a strategy, until over a lager one wet afternoon, in a strategy meeting with myself, I suppose – motivation's important – I'd picked up a copy of Heat magazine, which someone had left on a chair, by the bar. There was a story, plus photo, about an incident outside Stringfellows, involving Jade Goody. Jade Goody, the dear, the departed … Jade Goody, the published writer … it was then that I realised, in the manner of Kevin from *The Wonder Years*, that if I could somehow contrive to get onto Big Brother, that if I could do that myself, and also, crucially, not go mad in the process, then I might have some leverage with Harper Collins and so on when I came off the show. Well, it had to be worth a shot. At least, I'd rung up my agent and he'd seemed to think so.

'Yeah, why not?' he'd muttered, if not, admittedly, sounding all that confident about my chances of success. On a couple of levels.

And so it was that a few months later, I found myself entering the Big Brother house.

'Mike's from London, he's twenty eight, and he's a writer!' Davina shouted, as I stumbled out of the limo, and into the crowd. 'He says he wants to bring some culture into the house!'

The booing, it's true, was pretty much deafening. There were more than a few cries of 'wanker' thrown in. But you have to say something during the interviews, and after all, it had worked out. I'm still not sure how I got through the process – always be close to a couple of drinks, but not as many as ten, is the only advice I can usefully offer – but there it was anyway. A brief window of fame was within my grasp, just as long as I managed to keep things together.

I should explain about my gameplan. Which was fairly straightforward; just to bring up the novel whenever possible, and otherwise try to stay under the radar until about week four, when I'd be thrown out of the house in a dignified manner, as the sort of boffin the Big Brother voters never quite understand. And then talk about the book in the interview afterwards, as if in discussion with Melvyn Bragg. It was brilliant, I'd thought. Why had no one tried a stunt like this before?

The problem here, of course, was how to make sure that I went out early, without just quitting, thus missing my slot on eviction night. But that was the clever bit. That was where Lavender Bunny came in.

If you saw the series then you'll know all about him. You might even be wearing one of the t-shirts. But before he became who he is today, LB was officially in there as a keepsake from my girlfriend, doused as he was in her favourite perfume. I didn't have a girlfriend, of course, and LB, who had a zip in his back, was actually stuffed with emergency Valium, in case of tense situations, which were bound to crop up. But that was the story as we made our way in there, heavy swells down the staircase, through the luminous doorway, and into our time behind the shattered eyes.

Thirteen weeks later, we were still in the house, part of the last four on the final night. We couldn't possibly win, could we? On the one side sat Roy, Max and Juanita, packed tight and hugging on the sofas opposite, eyeing LB as if he was a striking cobra. And LB was giving them a hard stare back.

So it's fair to say the gameplan didn't work out. After a decade on prime-time TV, the show couldn't hope to command the attention it once had. But, on the internet message boards where these things are discussed, series ten's still considered a fairly good year. Certainly there was drama from day one on. There was sex, there was violence, there were all kinds of arguments, and really no shortage of big personalities. And that was what turned out to be the problem, in the end. Because how to get nominated, never mind evicted, if everyone else is a borderline lunatic? You prepare yourself for eccentric behaviour, that's what the show was about after all, but that year felt like a final roll of the dice on Channel Four's part. At times it seemed as if someone could have put up a burning cross on the lawn, and it would have been forgotten a day or so later, overtaken by events. In fact, I wouldn't be willing to swear that nobody tried it.

The first month went by easily enough, though. Each time there was a fight, and God knows there were many, Islam-gate, lager-gate, dirty-underwear-gate (not to ask about any of them, but especially not that one) LB and I would repair to the bedroom, and pop another sleeper.

He used to say to me;

'Mike, if we run out of this stuff we're in serious trouble.'

'Don't worry LB,' I'd reply, 'We'll be long gone before that happens.'

But of course, I was wrong. I'd packed enough pills for six weeks, worst-case scenario. But by the end of week four, I was already having to cut back drastically. Which meant I had to get involved in what was happening in the house, instead of just watching it, as if it was some kind of strange, catastrophic, scientific experiment.

What became clear, pretty quickly, was that people felt I'd been sitting on the fence. And that I had a gameplan. Plus an unhealthy relationship with – well, over to Roy, who was from Wolverhampton, I think about twenty, and possessed of an almost heroic sense of personal entitlement:

'Hey mate, is it part of being a writer's job to take a rabbit with you, like, everywhere, or what?'

'What.' I supposed.

'I mean, does Salman Rushdie have a frigging bunny, or what?'

This went on for a while. Waking up to a drug-free reality live on Channel Four . . . I just wouldn't advise it.

I had a heart to heart with LB in the bathroom, shortly after Roy's outburst.

'LB,' I said, 'What are we going to do about this?'

'Well Mike, it could be time for what we discussed.'

'Yeah. Is it going to work though?'

'I think so,' LB said. 'And then after this, can we go back home, Mike?'

'Of course we can, LB.'

'I just want to sit on the desk like I used to do Mike, and not have to see any of these people, ever again.'

'I understand.'

'All right then.'

The housemates were completing that week's shopping list, when LB first spoke up. The shopping list was always a bit of a low-point, especially if we were on a basic budget. After various upsets in the past, the producers weren't allowed to feed us booze the whole time, so what they'd do instead was engineer situations whereby everyone was on a short fuse, and liable to kick off at any moment, due to a lack of food. So compiling the shopping list would, as a task, take on this almost hallucinatory sense of gravitas. We'd been at it for nearly a hour by this point.

'Right then, we need to make sure we have enough frozen vegetables,' said Graham, who'd been involved in local government back in the real world, as was fairly clear from his manner, if not the Day-Glo, lycra cycling shorts he was currently sporting. At twenty-eight, I was a bit long in the tooth for all this, so what Graham, who was pushing forty, was doing on the show was anyone's guess. Working his way through some personal issues? So it seemed. Anyway, LB couldn't let this pass, so:

'No, we don't,' he said.

'I'm sorry?'

'Lavender Bunny says that he doesn't like frozen vegetables. He says they're for wankers.'

'Right,' said Graham, 'but given the, I think, incontrovertible fact that as an inanimate object, that rabbit doesn't eat food, his opinions are irrelevant. Now if we could get on . . .'

'He also says that those shorts are a disgrace.'

'Oh he does, does he?'

'I'm afraid so.'

'Well Michael, I think I'm entitled to make my own decisions about my apparel.'

'Lavender Bunny says he thinks the only thing you're entitled to is a smack in the mouth.'

'I see. Are you going to carry on like this, Michael?'

'Lavender Bunny says he thinks so, yes. He also thinks this food thing is a waste of time, and that we should get beer instead. And that now that Tiffany with the knockers has been voted out, we should exchange one of our tokens for a stripper.'

And so we went on. By the start of week seven, I'd stopped saying anything, trusting LB to do the necessary instead. And certainly, he stepped up to the plate in grand style By the time we arrived at the final night, he'd threatened to kill or at least seriously injure pretty much everyone in there. But I suppose, in a way, that's what we want from our housemates. It didn't seem to matter what he said, or how many times we were up for eviction (eight, I think, which must be some kind of record) nothing was enough to get us voted out. Which brings us back to the final night. There we were on the sofas, me, LB, Roy, Max and Juanita, waiting to hear who'd won the series. The tension was palpable.

'This is Davina!' shrieked the voice. 'Housemates, you are live on Channel Four, please do not swear.'

'Bollocks,' said LB.

First out was Max, and then Juanita. Which left Roy, who any other year might have cruised to victory, handsome chap as he was, and LB, and me. Seeing as LB had described Roy as 'a talking erection' on a couple of occasions, this time was characterised by an uncomfortable silence.

'If you win this, mate,' Roy hissed, 'it'll be a friggin' disgrace . . .'

'And the winner is . . . Lavender Bunny!'

Boos, cheers, 'We love LB!' and so on, ensued. The look of disgust on Roy's face was quite gratifying, to begin with, until it turned out that in LB, I had inadvertently created something of a monster.

'So, Mike, you've written a novel! I'm fascinated!' Davina didn't ask, in our exit interview. Instead, she was full of questions for a blushing LB, who rose to the occasion with great aplomb. And now he's a celebrity. Well, I don't begrudge him – after all, I go where he goes, to all the hot clubs. China White and Tiger Tiger and Strawberry Moon. And the book is coming out, and I'm a hundred grand richer. And we're doing all the magazines. Perhaps unsurprisingly, he's been a big hit with both *Nuts* and *Zoo,* posing for photos with the lovelies *du jour.* Perhaps *Hello* beckons next and the society pages of *The Daily Mail,* but the fact remains that for the foreseeable future, I'm basically going to be LB's plus one, as opposed to a serious literary figure.

Some days, my mind turns back to the great literary creations of the past, in particular to Coleridge's Ancient Mariner, and the albatross hanging around his neck, as he repeats his story to the guests at the party, over, and over, and over again . . . oh well.

ELEPHANTS' GRAVEYARD

So, my brothers, it was a bad situation. It was fucking bad, actually. I couldn't believe they'd just left me like that, the others. Well, I'm a big bloke, you know, I'm hardly inconspicuous, and yet there I was anyway, standing around like a prize bloody lemon in the arse-end of nowhere, with nothing but desert in any direction, as far as I could see. There was no pool, there was no caff, there were no proper facilities. In fact there didn't seem to be any sort of infrastructure, at all.

If going abroad's really all about home, and how much you'd miss it if you couldn't go back there, if that's at least one of the points of a foreign holiday, then it was a point, by then, that had been well fucking taken. I'd only gone off for a couple of minutes, to see about getting a drink of something, or maybe an ice lolly – anything to cool off a bit after God knows how many hours on that oven of a coach. No such luck, I hasten to add, so when I got back to the underwhelming sight of no bus, no loo and no fucking tour guides, as if they'd all buggered off to the hotel without me, the cunts.

As a holiday situation, it was hardly ideal.

So I must have stumbled along for a bit after that, like a big, sweaty bloke with a heart condition, like the proverbial

Englishman, in the midday sun. Until I got to the edge of what looked like a settlement, from which point I could see, well, not all that much. There was a truck-stop, a shed and a couple of soldiers, or maybe Old Bill. Whatever they were, they didn't seem friendly, necking warm beers in the afternoon heat, guns on their knees, eyes looking heavy, like dirty fried eggs. And then a bit further on there were shacks, some more shacks, and a few scratchy trees. Plus a goat, the odd chicken and some kids playing football with a skull, or something, the view untroubled by satellite dishes, or even any shops. God help me if I have to spend the night here, I thought, in the middle of Noddyland. And it was starting to get dark.

'See the world,' they'd said. 'Broaden your horizons. You're in a rut, mate.' And maybe I was. Perhaps life, after all, had been a bit too predictable back at home. It was the same old faces most of the time, at least apart from the tourists, and you'd get a shag, it's true, about once in a blue moon. But if life wasn't the great adventure the old blokes would talk about sometimes down at the watering hole, then at least it was comfortable. Not, in other words, like this sodding dump, where it seemed clear enough that whatever you do, you should never leave London, and especially not if you're relying on Thomas fucking clueless to get you back home again.

Still, they were sure to come after me, it stood to reason they would, and they were bound to find the village, sooner or later. So in a couple of weeks I'd be safely back home, having a *good old laugh* about my African holiday, I supposed. And it was really cold by now, and I was knackered, and starving, and I could hear the jackals, or lions, or whatever they were, howling up at the moon from somewhere nearby. So I decided to see about approaching the village, in the hope that the locals could sort me out.

Tentatively then, I moved away from the trees I'd been hiding in, trying to stay incognito – as I said earlier, I'm a fairly big bloke. I knew I must be a sight, lumbering out of the darkness, a bit unsteady on my pins. I was trying to make it clear that I wasn't a nutter, that I meant no harm, and that I was really just after some food and some water, and a place to lie down. Which, as you can probably see from my current condition, was a fucking big mistake. Because as I got closer the village went mental – that's the only way of putting it. There were shouts and screams, there was all this palaver, wild dogs crying in the night, the natives looking restless, rising up from around their oil can bonfires as one of the soldiers went for his weapon.

So there was a pain in my shoulder, bloody agony actually, and then a lot more shot flying over my ears as I turned tail and bolted, claret jetting everywhere. It's probably something you lot are used to, but I'd never known people to act like that. They might, where I'm from, try and slip you a beer on occasion, and their kids, the little fuckers, might sometimes stretch to a rotten apple, or an ice lolly packed with broken glass, but nothing worse than that . . . all in all, I don't mind admitting my eyes were a bit damp.

And after that, my brothers, things became strange.

They were bad days actually, when for various stretches I was off my rocker. I suppose I had visions, of palm trees, an oasis, stuff like that. I remembered the old blokes talking about it, back home, about somewhere they'd refer to as our ancestral graveyard, which some of us see when we're on our last legs, even if it's bollocks, a final trick of the mind. I never quite knew what they were getting at really, but out in the wasteland during that time I think I had glimpses. Of green plains, rock pools and our lot everywhere, like everything must have been, back in the old days.

I spoke to the spirits, or with some of the faces that live there now, who tried to set me straight on a couple of things. Such as, that I'd never been out there on holiday in the first place, and that the tour guides had left me on purpose, the cunts. That even though I know precisely fuck-all about how to survive out here, the plan was to 'voluntarily repatriate' me into the wild, like some sort of bell-end on a reality TV show. As I'm sure you can imagine, I was a bit gutted when I heard that. Well, they think we're just wankers, that we don't understand, as if English is something we couldn't pick up on, even though our brains are about three times the size. But even so, to be confronted with the evidence was a bit like catching one of the keepers stark bollock naked in the reptile house, approaching the snake pit, strides at half mast – you know they're all probably as mad as arseholes, but it's still a bit much to have to look at the evidence, all the same.

Eventually, I came across a pool with clean water, and some grub nearby I could just about eat, and where I could hose down the wound in my shoulder. But I don't know, really, I think it might have gone septic. I'm not feeling that clever now, certainly. And I wasn't feeling much better back then, when the film crew arrived. I was lying in the mud when the trucks pulled up like another mirage, the BBC logo bright in the sun. At last I thought, although fairly delirious – they looked like saints in their damp, dusty t-shirts and holiday beards – I'll get some sense out of this lot, they'll give me a shot, try and bandage my shoulder, even stretcher me out of here, back to civilisation. But no. It was against the cunts' principles to intervene, it seemed. So instead they just filmed me stumbling about, as if I was some wanker on the beers down in Camden market.

And then they packed up the cameras and left me to it. Believe it or not, I actually overheard a couple of them discussing 'the pathos of the situation'. Which was a bit much, seeing as those pitiless, environmentalist, trust fund cock rings were all that seemed to stand between me and extinction, personally. It just wasn't the sort of thing that would have happened in London – when one of us blokes is in a bad way back there, what they usually do is start an appeal.

So then you lot turned up, my African brothers, although I dare say you can't understand a word of what I'm on about. That I'm wasting what little breath I have left. 'Cunts', 'Bollocks', 'Wankers' . . . these, sadly, will be my final words. The ancient cemetery seems close, very close, to this terrible shitter my erstwhile attendants have seen fit to dump me in. Did they think I was a jaffa, or something? Must have done, I suppose. But I was doing my best back there, really I was. I was the friendliest elephant in the zoo, for Christ's sake. I had great things ahead of me, perhaps even telly, and look at me now. Too banged-up to be on David Attenborough, and lying here gazing up at the bright, flying visions of the life to come, like in Dumbo basically, though with vultures hovering, as opposed to crows, what do I think about this? About being set free, in a way?

I think, honestly, that my erstwhile captors were labouring under a misapprehension. I think they thought they were having a fucking giraffe.

PETE DOHERTY'S CHRISTMAS CAROL

About my relationship with the city of Norwich, prior to the events of the evening in question, I will say very little, because I didn't really have one.

We'd been booked to play there often enough, me and the guys from the band. It was a major stop on the college tour circuit, and in that sense, unmissable. But, seeing as on three separate occasions in the last year we'd managed to do just that, to miss it, that is, once because of problems with snow on the motorway (this is not a euphemism for taking heroin), once because of the monkey on our drummer's back (again, this isn't a euphemism for taking heroin. He'd had to have stitches, poor bloke, after an incident at Chessington zoo that, thankfully, hadn't made it as far as the national press) and once because I'd forgotten all about it, still at home 'working on my novel' when we were due on stage, (which was a euphemism for taking heroin, though I'd accepted an advance from Harper Collins, all the same) it seemed safe to assume that relations between me and my fans in Norwich weren't all they might have been. And that was equally true of sales of our album there. At one point, the figure of twelve was being bandied about. Even allowing for mitigating factors, that seemed enough to have anyone reaching for the laudanum, really. Well, or maybe people were downloading it, I don't know. Either way, I'd done a lot of work on my novel after hearing that.

So perhaps it was a feeling of guilt that drove me to Norwich, on that fateful Christmas Eve. It seems unlikely, but you never know. Or at least I don't, anyway. Famously, I guess, I try to keep a diary, but those of you who've seen the published volume will be familiar with the problem, that, as a prose piece, it's quite experimental, as if a ink-stained spider's been turned loose on the page, after a large belt of blotter acid.

Still, it's a nice object, I like to think. And even if it isn't, that was what I'd agreed to go to Norwich to promote, at my editor's uncle's bookshop. Well I owed my editor a few favours, as I'm sure you can imagine.

They'd suggested I do a reading at first, but that might have been tricky, so what I'd said I'd do instead was play a short acoustic set, then sign some copies. No doubt illegibly, but there you go. It wasn't as if I had much else to do. The situation between me and the London police was such that even a trip to the cornershop felt like a Benny Hill chase sketch, as reimagined by William Burroughs. As for Christmas at home, well, I still hadn't forgiven Mum for writing that book about me. Which isn't a euphemism for taking heroin, although I rather wished it had been. So thumbs down, basically, to the idea of a traditional Christmas. If anyone had asked me what I thought about that, I might well have replied 'Bah, humbug!'

And if you're going to be lonesome, why not in Norwich?

By two o'clock then, when Bob, my PA, finally bundled me into the Jag, we were already a bit late. I hadn't heard, or perhaps even set, my alarm, so Bob, as we moved off into heavy traffic, the snow already falling hard, was tight-lipped in the rearview mirror.

And only more so by the time we parked in front of the bookshop, which, by then, had been shut for an hour. On the door, somebody had pinned a sign reading 'Fuck off Doherty' so I'd signed that, at least.

'So what are we going to do now Bob?'

'Well, let's see,' said Bob. 'Play a few songs outside the cathedral? *What A Waster* might be good.'

'I'm sensing some hostility here, Bob.'

'Oh *are* you?'

'I stand, Bob, for the spirit of Merrie Olde England,' I reminded him, 'not all this commercialism'.

'I think I might have enjoyed being violated by festive capitalism more if I was at home with my partner.'

'Who, Tiny Tim?'

'One of the reasons you hired me, Pete, is that I have a black belt in karate. I suggest you remember that.'

'Yeah . . . anyway, maybe we should see about getting a hotel?'

'What?'

'Well, can you face driving back through that blizzard?'

'Both inside the car, and out. No, I suppose not,' Bob relented, 'but I'm having the penthouse suite. And you're buying the drinks. Because should I, Pete, be working on Christmas Eve? What would the NME make of all this? From their erstwhile Coolest Man of the Year?'

'Let's not get into that again, Bob.'

Much, much later, I came sailing out of the elevator, in wherever it was we were staying that night. Bit blurry by this point, I'd had a few, although not so many that it wasn't still something of a surprise when the door of my room began to talk back to me. 'Hello, hello, hello', it seemed to sing, in a low, dolorous moan. But the corridor was empty, there was no one about, Bob having passed out during a crying jag a few hours earlier. Probably, someone had spiked my last Sambuca, so the first thing I did, after putting on MTV, was chop out a line of something soothing. And then I started to see about raiding the minibar. At £350 a night, the last thing you want to do in a place like that is sleep, really.

It was then that the first ghost appeared. Clutching a shotgun and a used syringe, it emerged, long-haired, from the television, dressed in Levis and a blood-stained pair of Converse, bandaged about the head. Quite an alarming sight, in principle, but equally, as a long-time fan of recreational pharmacopoeia, I was quite used to this sort of thing.

'Kurt?' I said. 'All right?'

'I guess not, man.'

'Oh. Would you like some of this?'

The spectre emitted a bloodcurdling wail.

'That's why I'm here, man. You've gotta get off the junk.'

'Yeah ... I used to get this off Kate the whole time though. What good did it do?'

'I hear ya,' Kurt muttered. 'Look, you've read the book, right? So here's the deal. Tonight you'll be visited by three spirits.'

'Excellent. Alistair Sim and all that.'

'No man, you don't understand. I'm in eternal torment.'

'Are you? That seems a bit rough. I've always thought *Nirvana Unplugged* was a great album. You haven't *actually* gone to the lake of fire, have you?'

Another scream.

'I mean, at least you weren't like Sting or Bono, droning on about charity the whole time ...'

A deafening howl at this point.

'But I should have been! Charity was my business. I should have been headlining Live Aid Two.'

'I did play that, though.'

'Dude, you were seriously fucked up.'

'But at least I *turned* up ... and you'd have shot yourself, honestly, if you'd been on that bill . . .'

'Oh wordly man . . .' wailed the spirit.

'All right, I could have put that better. But could you keep it down a bit? That is, assuming you ain't just a crumb of Lebanese black I swallowed earlier, by a mistake . . .'

There were further dolorous groans.

'Man, before you dismiss me as a bad trip, I've gotta tell you, there's a place in heaven for Phil Collins and those assholes from U2. Whereas conversely . . .'

At this point Kurt threw open the window, to reveal Johnny Thunders, Sid Vicious, Jim Morrison and others, floating around by the charity muggers, trying to intervene.

'Some of us,' said Kurt, unwinding the bandage around his head (what with the gunshot injury, it wasn't a pretty sight) 'are otherwise occupied. So I got you a pass, man. Just try and listen to what the ghosts have to say.'

'But why me? ' I said.

'Nothing better to do, I guess.'

'Oh. Yeah . . . cool.'

I don't know what time it was when the second knock came, but I was reasonably sure I hadn't hired anyone from an escort agency. Did they even have those in Norwich? If you're the singer in a cult indie band, someone else usually handles that kind of thing. Anyway, I opened the door. Or is that right? Perhaps the ghost just materialised while I was lying on the bed, thinking of sleigh bells and reindeer and so on, floating away in a starry sky.

The figure outside was short and blonde. I may as well say she looked a bit like Kate (Moss, for those of you who've been out the game lately – though physician heal thyself, I suppose) and so consequently, was plausibly somebody I might have asked to keep me company, over the phone.

Basically, if you're ever in this situation, it's best not to prepare a thingummy, shall we say, before you've established what's going on. Particularly when a vortex seems manifest, over the minibar. As the drugs hero of my generation (there's no real competition, is there? Those guys from Oasis? From Blur? I think not) I was pretty used to this sort of thing. But still, being dragged back in time by a pixie from an agency, probably, was new. If I had my time over again, I'm not sure I'd have pressed the plunger when I did.

This was to prove to be a theme. Anyway, an earlier Christmas when I'd been gigging with The Libertines, and Carl was still in the band. I haven't got much to say about this. Yes, all right, we could have been more successful if I'd been less difficult about things (I saw myself huffing away on a makeshift crack-pipe in the Gents, before phoning my lawyer, and then, horrendously, Elton John) but life is short, and you have to keep moving. As I explained to what was presumably the ghost of Christmas Past, who very much resembled Nikki from Big Brother, if you remember her. I barely did myself, but I'd apparently once hired her, back when she worked for 'Angels Of Islington'. Allegedly, I'd been unable to rise to the occasion – it was in the Sundays at the time. Anyway, she hadn't changed much. I received a stern lecture about heroin and cocaine, but at this point in my career, I was used to a few of those, on a daily basis. The ghosts were going to have to try harder.

Although saying that, I think I already had some idea of what was coming next.

I was drifting off to sleep when it arrived though, this ragged, grey-haired figure in a Santa suit.

'Give me your fucking money!' it demanded, in a grating Irish accent, 'Don't go to the pub tonight, just give me your fucking money.'

'Yeah . . .' I heard myself saying, as, without further ado, I was enveloped in the fetid, red cloak of the ghost of Christmas Present, or Bob Geldof, if you'd rather, and taken on a whistle-stop tour of what a swine I was, as an employer; 'Tiny' Tim, Bob my PA's partner, who was actually a fifteen-stone weightlifter from Bondi Beach, would be gone by next year, leaving only his surfboard by Bob's fireplace, if I carried on paying Bob such lousy wages.

'Fair enough,' I said. Not, and I should have realised this, that my forbearance on the subject was likely to stop this particular aspect of the ghost of Christmas Present from opening his robe up, to reveal the starving children beneath. And also, if inadvertently, (I had to hope) his old chap and testicles.

'Poverty! And Ignorance!' Bob yelled. 'Look at them!'

So I was still a bit shaken, and hunched over the minibar, when the spirit of Christmas Future arrived, with its hood and its scythe, to whisk me off to the site of my Chatterton-esque resting place. It was cold and grey, and rather bleak, but, 'Oh well,' I supposed, 'Oscar Wilde's headstone isn't that big either. And I've always fancied an early death.'

With its skeletal hand, the spirit pointed out the inscription. Which didn't mention my poetry or music at all, instead just stating 'Pete Doherty 1979-2057.'

'2057?' I said. 'But that means . . . no, that can't be right . . .'

Again the spectre waved its claw at my grave. Which next read;

'Beloved father to Kevin, Cosmo, and Keith. Beloved husband to Lily Allen.'

'Oh. Oh no . . .'

The next morning, I leapt out of bed, past the empties and so on, with a new sense of purpose. I would clean up my act, keep Christmas better, and stop wasting away in provincial hotels. Full of the joys of the season then, I rang up room service, asked to speak to the manager, and offered to treat the good folk of Norwich to a festive sing-song, in the hotel bar.

'Yes. Well, we appreciate the gesture, Mr. Doherty, but Christmas ended several days ago. And there's the matter of your bill.'

'Oh,' I said, as the bloke read out the itemised total, eight bottles of brandy, a few of gin, a hundred beers and twenty KitKats ('for the foil' I'd apparently yelled, repeatedly), 'Fucking humbug . . .'

TRIES TO COOK AND EAT GORDON RAMSAY

First off, I have to make one thing clear: I am not a chef. I'd like to be, of course. Who wouldn't these days? The industry's come a long way since the years of Fanny Craddock and the Muppet Show's Swede. To the point where now, the kind of guy who might once have been accused of being tied to his mother's apron can reasonably look forward to his own TV series by the time he's thirty. To say nothing of the book deals, and the international jet-set lifestyle. Look at Jamie Oliver, for example. Well, *you* look at him – I can't, really, without imagining a pig shitting on his head.

But enough about Oliver. The man I'm here to talk to you about is Gordon Ramsay, who for various reasons I'm about to relate I recently crossed swords with, and kitchen knives, in a way that likely means he won't be running any more marathons, at least for a while.

Because business is business. And business is something I do know about. I may not know much about pleasing a woman (in fact, I'm probably more of an expert in the opposite of that) but investment capital is a part of my skill-set. And you do get tired of the daily grind, hence my decision, last Christmas, to leave my position at Goldman

Sachs and get into the restaurant game instead. I mean I liked food, I ate it, what could possibly go wrong?

Well as it turned out, virtually everything. The Pozzo dei Soldi was a lovely little place in Soho where my ex-wife and I (I'm not prepared to discuss this, but the break-up was . . . complicated) had been going for years. We'd had our first date there in 1985, where I introduced her to the rigatoni al forno and the amazing prosciutto. In 1989 I proposed to her with Giulio, the owner and head chef, looking on, and we've been back for our anniversary every year since. In 2006, I'd put rat poison in her carbonara – result there, incidentally, but I probably shouldn't be telling you that.

Anyway, seeing as I was ready, after twenty-odd, high-achieving years, to resign from my position at Goldman Sachs, when I heard that Giulio was in trouble with various creditors, I naturally offered to step in. A place like that, in that location, with thirty years of goodwill behind it, was a solid-gold investment opportunity, surely?

Well yes, and no. It took me just over a week to realise that there was something rotten in the state of the Pozzo, over and above the food. Although that had rather gone off in recent years too. There was a family of rats living in the wine cellar, and Giulio, it turned out, was an inveterate lush, obsessed with hard drugs to the point of being totally unable to put together even a basic ragu, without recourse to his own, very private salt shaker ; his idea of sourcing local ingredients was . . . well this was Soho. And his wife Francesca was even more committed to the cause. First night in she pulled up her sleeve, showed me her track-marks, then collapsed on the kitchen floor, babbling about Madonna. Or the Madonna, I suppose it might have been. Either way, not good. And about the second chef Alberto's leisure time antics, I simply refuse to comment.

So the goose that laid the golden eggs had turned out, instead, to be an impotent gander, shitting money on the floor. Problem was, I hadn't a bloody clue what to do about it. This went on for a while.

Until Francesca, presumably after an especially heavy, night-off session, mentioned a series called Kitchen Nightmares, presented by Gordon Ramsay. The premise was that the blustering cock himself would descend on a restaurant that was going arse-up, fire the staff, rip out the fixtures and change the menu, and hey presto, in four weeks it's gone from haemorrhaging cash to turning people away. And it gets a primetime advert on national TV into the bargain.

Well it had to be worth a shot, so I gave the producers a call. Long story short, they decided the place was perfect, (a perfect disaster, that was) and filming could begin in a month. They were going to make it their Easter special, they said. And Gordon Ramsay was to be our redeemer.

The first few days went by quietly enough. To get the lowdown on Ramsay, I'd watched a few episodes of his show, so I knew well enough to play the good-hearted amateur, and stay out of his way while he worked his magic. And Ramsay, to be fair, was no slacker. He bollocked the kitchen, he flirted with the waitresses, he called Alberto an arsehole and promoted Louis, our work-experience fuck of a sous chef to a position well above his station. Of course, there were a couple of hitches, such as Giulio threatening to kill himself when Gordon ripped out the original Seventies décor and went at the walls with a bucket of Farrow & Ball, but he saw sense eventually. And fuck him, actually. Fuck Giulio. If the hopeless dope fiend had been more business-smart, none of us would have been in this mess in the first place.

On day three, the name was changed (without my consent) to Paparazzo.

'Paparazzo?' I wondered, staring furiously up at the new sign, hovering over the door.

'It's funky,' he said. 'Modern. Cutting-edge. This the

twenty-first century, big boy, not fucking 1973.'

Next, he threw out all the pasta, in much the same way as he'd evicted the rats, and created a new menu of what he called 'pan-Continental-Tex-Mex-Asian-fusion'. Which wouldn't have been quite so bad if he hadn't also insisted we use fresh, organic, locally-sourced ingredients.

'Where Gordon,' I asked, 'am I going to get British-grown jalapeno and organic octopus?'

'Borough Market,' he replied, with a strange look in his eye. 'They've got everything there.'

'Right.' I sighed. 'Well, you're the boss.'

Tellingly perhaps, he did not disagree. But all the same, I'd say the real trouble didn't start until the second week of filming, on the night of Paparazzo's grand re-opening.

I arrived there late, because I'd had a few whiskies the evening before, after a crisis meeting with my now-hated bank manager, when he'd informed me they were about to foreclose, because of interest from elsewhere. And then the first sight that greeted me was a weepy Francesca, heading into the Ladies with a meaningful look.

'Francesca,' I said, as I followed her in there. 'It's the re-launch tonight. If you OD on camera we'll never hear the end of it.'

She rolled her smoky, pinned-out, Latina eyes. 'Dave, I do anything . . . but please do not make me speak to that son-of-a-whore again. He insult my work, he insult my family, and he has a face like a fucking warthog.'

'Yes, but money talks, and right now it's saying that we need Gordon to pull our arses out of the fire, I'm afraid. *Capisce?*'

She glared at me darkly, crossed herself, and left.

As did I, heading into the kitchen, where emotions I supposed, were bound to be running quite high, as they're supposed to in a working restaurant. Even so, should Giulio have been standing there trembling, apparently about to set about Ramsay with a squid-stuffed turkey, basted in red pepper sauce?'

Well, no. Thinking about how all this was going to look on television – ghastly, of course, there was no way round it – I leapt into the fray.

'Erm, could you chill out guys? Don't get blood on the walls anyway,' I joked, 'that new paint's expensive, ha ha! Now, what's all this about?'

'He say my melanzano taste like a toddler's shit, the fucking bastard. How do he know what that taste like, eh?'

'Mate,' said Gordon, 'you fucking know it's true . . . he's a fucking liability, Dave!' he continued, turning to me. 'He shouldn't even be here, the knob! His noisettes de veau look like someone's got their fucking cock out on them! Tell him!'

'Come on Giulio,' I supposed, 'maybe you are a bit old for this now?'

'Fuck you! My father die in his kitchen, age eighty-nine! Face down in a pot of linguini!'

'Congratulations,' I said, at a loss.

'Shit on this,' said Gordon, knocking the bird from the junkie cook's shaking hand, hitting him hard in the jaw and then wrestling him, facedown, onto the stove. 'Come on big boy,' said the bringer of nightmares to a million British kitchens. 'Where are your fucking bollocks?'

'Dave,' squeaked Giulio into the hot-plate. 'I no longer put up with this. If he stays, I go.'

'Well if he stays, I fucking go,' countered Gordon.

'Hang on guys,' I said desperately, 'Can't we just, you know, take five and think things over?'

Everyone looked at me like I'd suggested they blow Gary Rhodes. Then Ramsay frogmarched Giulio out of the kitchen.

After that, things went rapidly downhill.

The re-launch, of course, was a glowing success. After the departure of Giulio and Francesca, an energised Gordon stepped into the breach, both helming the kitchen, and, perhaps more importantly, drawing on his PR's list of contacts to make Paparazzo's opening an event that was truly worthy of its name. The glitterati of theatre land attended in style: Jason Donovan, Martine McCutcheon, Christian Slater, it was a night to remember.

None of which, sadly, was enough to save the place. Deprived of the oxygen of the Ramsay name, and serving up food that was really pretty awful (why, I sometimes wondered, had Gordon suggested that menu?) Paparazzo shut down in the dog days of May, apparently tough in the restaurant trade.

So all that remained was the follow-up interview, when the Nightmares team checks back on the place.

We'd been closed for a week then, but I still had the keys, though already there was a sign outside that read 'Under New Management'. So after a consultation with my old pal Johnnie Walker, it seemed the only thing to do was confront Gordon man-to-man, in Paparazzo's kitchen.

To give him his due, he was reasonably conciliatory – often he lays into 'Nightmares' failures for screwing the pooch, but this time he limited himself to observing that some people just aren't cut out for the restaurant biz. I was eyeing a meat cleaver at the time, and as he made this last observation, it suddenly occurred to me how much more interesting his wrinkled, pink head might look if it was steaming on a platter, with an apple in its mouth.

I picked up the chopper and advanced towards him.

'Paparazzo?' I seethed. 'Whale-meat enchiladas? Dean Gaffney at the opening? You must think I was born fucking yesterday!'

'Showing some bollocks at last, eh?'

'I'd be careful how I phrased that if I were you, Gordon.'

'But come on Dave,' blustered Gordon. 'All's fair in business and war. And I've always fancied a little bistro in

Soho. And you can't make an omelette without breaking a few eggs.'

'But I'm not making an omelette, Gordon,' I said. 'A pork dish was more what I had in mind. With extremely fresh and locally-fucking-sourced ingredients . . .'

I think, as I lunged at him with the blade, and the first lovely jet of blood went splattering onto the kitchen wall, I was actually slavering.

'You'll never get away with this, big boy,' Gordon croaked, his face now the off-yellow shade of factory farmed chicken, as the film crew looked on, aghast.

'Oh come on, Gordon,' I said, as I belted him about the side of the head with the end of the cleaver, forced him back onto the stainless steel counter, and set about slitting him open for offal. 'It's fucking brilliant publicity for the new place. Right?'

THE NOTTING HILL PUNISHER

How is all this going to end? It's difficult to say. It's quite a strange business, watching the cops start blocking the end of your road off live on News 24, while on the screen, there's all this talk of a crazy, lone gunman.

As situations go, it isn't like a meeting with senior management, or the other side in a business deal. Because while those can feel tense, and often quite threatening, and you might well think you'd like to start shooting, there's no real chance of that actually happening. I mean, you try taking a gun into work these days. Not that you should, of course, but when I first started out it used to seem doable. If it looked like there might be problems with a client, or I was due to discuss my appraisal or something, I used to pack my old revolver with my lunch in my briefcase. Not to use it, obviously, so much as just have it there for moral support, or as a confidence-booster, in the same sort of way you'd wear a lucky tie, perhaps, or a pair of Arsenal boxer shorts.

But that was in a more liberal time. Nowadays, it's as much as you can do to get a letter knife past Human Resources. In fact at my place, you can't even do that. There was a paperweight amnesty at the office a while ago, on the strength of the idea that in the world of e-commerce, any stationery that might be considered an offensive weapon is now redundant. I'd have begged to differ, but best, I thought, not to draw much attention to the state of Old Faithful, which was perhaps a bit sharper than strictly necessary for opening the post.

So propped up here behind the bedroom furniture, with the garden trip-wired to the best of my ability (this involves frozen orange juice, lighter fuel and a mobile phone, but it's probably best if I don't explain – I'm sure it's on the internet, if you're all that interested) what I'm mainly wondering is, am I successful enough? It's the key question – am I, or realistically *was* I earning enough? Did my colleagues *really* respect me? Or will they, when interviewed, just say I was one of those quiet types?

Because conceivably, if I don't start shooting now, I might just be carted away to a open facility for professional guys of a certain age, you know, for a while, as a token slap on the wrist. As long as my work record's solid, the judge may conceivably go for a plea of temporary insanity. I haven't actually killed anybody, after all. Not through lack of trying, it's true, but who's going to weep for their crack house? Or even the charity shop that did admittedly, rather get in the way? Won't anyone with even the most basic interest in property values understand why such outfits can be a negative? And that applies, I think, to charity shop in particular. Up to a point, the odd discreet vice den can add a certain amount of character, but what's the use of a Help The Aged? Like a pack of wild dogs, these places more or less target weak retail areas, where the ground rents are cheap, so by their very existence, aren't they lowering the tone? So won't Notting Hill be a more desirable post code with one less, at least? In a sense, haven't I done the street a favour? No, I'm not convinced either, but perhaps the courts will see it that way. And overlook the ash heap in Ladbroke Grove. Because everyone makes mistakes, every now and again.

Plus I did serve my country in Afghanistan, and later Iraq. I didn't mean to, exactly, I thought I'd sign up, get paid through college, and then just square bash for a couple of years, before settling down to a job in the City. I figured that after the Balkans, we'd lay off for a bit. Big mistake, that, but who, apart from the CIA, the FBI and the various embassies, could have predicted 9/11? Not me anyway. So I wasn't really expecting to end my tour of duty with at least a semi-expert understanding of the many interesting ways in which you can joint a man, with a butter knife or something. I've never been that good at anything much, but it turned out I was good at this. Some sort of promise was detected quite early during my training, so later, there were various black ops with special forces, and . . . well, in this case literally, the less said the better.

So as you may or may not have gathered, I was more or less a drooling lunatic by the time I finished my tour. When I looked in the mirror, all I'd see was a trained maniac, who was always going to know, because it's a bit like learning to ride a bike, exactly how to finish off everyone in the room. It was my bad luck, you could say, to have joined the British Army on 'Bomber' Blair's watch. 'Bomber' Blair being someone who'd have sent troops, apparently, to 'sort out' the statues on Easter Island if they'd looked at him funny, or hadn't make the right noises, or if the Bush Jr. government had told him to do it. I don't particularly want to get into the politics, what's done is done, but in the years that followed, I'd sometimes find myself reaching for my revolver, if he happened to pop up on the ten o'clock news.

Anyway my finger's on the trigger, and the mobile keypad is close to hand. And the police, hilariously, are circling the garden. What sort of chance do they think they have? I'm quite tempted to mow a few of them down as a matter of principle. Because fairly obviously, none of them have ever seen combat. It's actually quite embarrassing to watch. What do they think they're playing at, crab-walking around like drunks at a wedding, onto a lawn they must know is booby-trapped, unless they can't read the sign? Or do they think it's a joke? If so, they're about to be roughly disabused of that notion. I suppose I should probably stop them.

Seeing as fighting the cops . . . well it's not a good look for an old soldier. And I did, in all fairness, lay on this reception for the local Yardies.

Anyway I should explain about The Punisher, as you may not be familiar. Frank Castle, the original Punisher, was a comic book vigilante who first appeared in the early Seventies. He started out fighting Spider-Man, but soon went on to bigger things. There was a film starring Dolph Lundgren in the Eighties, and another one a couple of years ago. And you might have seen the t-shirt, a white skull on black – simple, iconic, and I'm wearing one now. But enough of the fashion tips. Frank was part of the sub-genre that gave rise to 'Taxi Driver', Clint Eastwood's turn as Dirty Harry, and then later the Rambo films. Dangerous guys in the post-Vietnam landscape, was the general idea. So Frank, in any case, was an ex-Marine who, back home after 'Nam, began another, much more personal war with the criminal element. His family, it's true, was wiped out by the mafia, but later iterations of the character (and after thirty years he's still going strong, so there must be a sort of enduring appeal) have portrayed that as an excuse, more than anything else, for Frank to get back to doing what he loved. Because while you can take the man out of special forces, you can't take the special forces out of the man.

It's a dilemma I can identify with. I don't know how common this is (obviously not very, or London, Manchester, Edinburgh . . . they'd all look a bit like Baghdad at this point) but I found it quite hard to forget my training. I don't know how anyone manages, really. In the queue at the supermarket, in meetings at work, in every frustrating situation that civilian life threw at me, which were, after all, just the same ones it throws at you, always inside there was the voice of the old soldier, eerily, icily calm, saying;

'Kill, Jim. Kill.'

And I was just so tired of having my car broken into. So the third time that happened in the same month, when I was woken up by the plaintive keening of my Lexus from the pavement outside, I suppose I went into a bit of a frenzy.

I was sleeping in the front room when it happened, camped out on the sofa, guns lined up on the coffee table. I shouldn't, by rights, still have had these, you're supposed to hand in your kit when you leave the service, but you pick up the odd thing during your travels, and I think most of us like to keep a few souvenirs. Especially if they know where the bodies are buried, which I did, and if they've been decorated, which I had. So I was out of the door in ten seconds flat, AK in one hand, pistol in the other, and instantly, gloriously, back in Basra, back in Kabul. After eight years in the City I was a bit out of shape, so the local youth who'd lifted my car stereo were a few streets away by the time I caught up with them. In fact by the time I came wheezing around the corner, they'd managed to cross into Ladbroke Grove, and were now outside what seemed uncomfortably like the neighbourhood crack house, where the residents weren't short of a few guns themselves. Oops.

They came piling out the door, the Yardies, like a cloud of angry wasps. Looking at what they were wearing, all that bling, I was quite tempted to put a few of them out of their misery, but no, just warning shots, I thought. Aim high, old soldier. I didn't want to risk shooting any civilians, the resting call girls and ex-public schoolboys who were stumbling out after them, looking dazed, a bit shaken, as you would, I suppose. Plus there was the question of property values. Part of the (with hindsight, crazy) plan had been to help keep those buoyant, by cleaning the scum off of West London's streets, but on reflection, turning the crescent into a war zone didn't seem likely to help out too much there.

Which was never more true than when, in full flight now, a handful of Yardies screaming blue murder on that leafy, well-appointed, West London terrace, I lobbed back a stun grenade to cover my exit. Horrendously, because I was rusty (every account I've managed, every long lunch I'd had, came back to haunt me then) the bomb veered slightly off to the left, then bounced the top of somebody's Range Rover, and, from there, with the ominous force of a Greek tragedy, or classic Stallone movie, into the window of Help The Aged. Which went up like the Fourth of July, on account, I suppose, of all the flammable tat. Did I mind? Yes and no. The explosion got the last few Yardies off my tail, but seeing as by this stage we were just round the corner from where I lived, it seemed that all that remained was for me to go back home, put on News 24, and prepare for reprisals.

As a war on crime, it was a bit ill-considered. In Iraq, I did much worse, and got medals for most of it, but there's no point pondering the irony now. I've got two options it seems, and not much time, at least judging by the coverage, live on TV. It's pretty disturbing, watching the snipers line up on the terrace, behind the cars banked opposite, the BMW's and so on. These days, are the police even trained to end a siege situation without killing everyone? With all the firepower on display, it doesn't seem likely.

And what would I be without a West London post code? Because whatever else happens, I will have to move. And can I go back to accountancy now? Not at at the same place obviously, that's a given, but generally? It's a definite 'no' from the inner old soldier – civilian life, he thinks, has never quite suited me. And am I really going to let these amateurs lock me away? Or instead go out in a blaze of glory?

It's a bit of a facer. Honestly, what would you do?

LAVENDER BUNNY AND CELEBRITY COME DINE WITH ME

Fame, fatal fame.

To be fair, everyone said that it wouldn't last. In fact for the final few weeks, nobody seemed to talk about anything else. It got so that by the end, Lavender Bunny and I could hardly face Stringfellows, it was as if Death himself was following us around, or sitting at our table in the VIP area, meaningfully eyeing the other celebs. Ah Stringfellows! Glorious Stringfellows! Would we never again sip its comp champagne? It was a worry.

Because chopping out lines with the day's glitterati can spoil you a bit for the local pub. So it's a difficult moment when your time runs out, when the bouncers inform you that from now on, mate, you'll have to pay on the door, like all the regular punters. As an aspiring writer, I was used to disappointment, but Lavender Bunny, who'd perhaps had his head turned more than even I knew, by his time in the back rooms of London's hot spots, was fairly inconsolable.

'Mike,' he used to say to me, 'Why do we never see Jodie Marsh no more?'

And;

'She said she loved me, Mike.'

And, perhaps inevitably;

'This is all *your* fault Mike!'

He took to drinking, he took to cocaine. He took to pacing the flat at all hours of the night, ranting about his agent. Well, I knew the feeling, but what could I tell him? He was only a small bunny, after all. I could have explained that we were really just mayflies, he and I. That there was a kind of terrible symmetry between the thirteen weeks we'd spent on television, and our thirteen weeks as Z-list celebs. That Peaches Geldof, Duncan from Blue, Dizzee Rascal and the rest of our set were just going to be people we saw in the papers, from now on. But I didn't have the heart. I didn't want to put out the hopeful light in his button-black eyes.

So, I suppose the last time we talked, LB and I had just won Big Brother, and were tabloid darlings. Or at least, LB was. I was just about to publish *Beer, Football And Shagging*, my debut novel, which had come out to decidedly ... mixed reviews. There seemed to be a feeling (and I'm really not saying this to try and sound interesting) that the world of letters had been waiting around for someone like me. That because we'd been on Big Brother, LB and I, trying to give the old novel a shot in the arm, I had no right to consider myself a serious artist. A lot of resentment came flooding out then, about Jordan, Jade Goody and other untouchable, best-selling writers. Perhaps I should have been flattered by some of the big beasts involved, but equally, there *is* such a thing as bad publicity. For example, Will Self said, and I quote, that it was 'an extremely accomplished debut, if, as one imagines, it was in fact penned by the author's rabbit', Jeanette Winterson called me 'a bloody idiot' and John Prescott, moonlighting as a critic for the Independent On Sunday, accused *me* of being 'untalented'.

'Mike,' said LB, when I read him the reviews, 'is Prescott the reason we never go out no more?'

'Well, he is the voice of the man on the street.'

'Oh. And what about Janet Waterstones? Who's she?'

I explained, briefly.

'But Mike, wouldn't she like me if she met me?'

'I'm sure she would, LB. But she isn't like Candy and Bambi from Babes Of Mayfair.'

'But Mike . . .'

'No LB, she isn't . . . at least, I'm pretty sure she isn't.'

So there we were, cast out of Stringfellows, shunned by the literary world, and effectively washed up by Christmas of the year of our Big Brother victory. Fame had been sweet, but it did have an after-taste. Sometimes, I'd catch LB in front of *Hollyoaks* or *The X Factor*, eyeing the screen like a man in torment. He wasn't going to be his old self again until we were back in the high life, that much was clear.

So what were our options? Well, they weren't that extensive. *I'm A Celebrity Get Me Out Of Here* was literally out, because, as I explained to LB, I'd be the one who was force-fed the testicles by the great British public, and not him.

'But Mike . . .'

'LB, we're not going on that during a recession. It just wouldn't be good.'

'What's a recession, Mike?'

'It's something, LB, that makes a lot of people very angry. And liable to take out their feelings of rage and frustration on such gilded creatures as you and I. So me, effectively.'

'But Mike, don't you love me no more?'

'Of course I do, LB. But you have to trust me on this.'

'But Mike,' he said, giving me a hard stare, 'what if I don't?'

So phew, then, I thought, when the call came through from McTavish, our theatrical agent, and we were offered a slot on *Celebrity Come Dine With Me*. If you haven't seen it, the format's simple. Four famous-ish faces take turns to host a dinner party, and score each other's performance, in terms of food, hosting and entertainment, out of ten. The winner earns a thousand pounds for their favourite charity, and perhaps a bit of a leg-up for their ailing career, and . . . that's it, pretty much.

The advantage of this was that, unlike Big Brother, it's repeated a lot, so in that sense, LB and I would be immortalised, at least for a while, if in the more obscure backwaters of Channel 4's schedule. Plus, Peter Stringfellow had been on the show, so could he deny us access to his VIP area after we'd done the same, without being forced to question his own celebrity, and thus reason for being? I was hoping not.

Jason Donovan, Jodie Marsh, John Prescott and us, then, was the line-up for the week.

'I'm looking forward to seeing Jodie again, Mike! And I want to meet Prescott.'

'Me too, LB.' I said, glad to see him happy again, if reflecting on the time, now long since past, when I could just about keep him under control.

So night one, which took place at Jason Donovan's lovely home in Ladbroke Grove.

On the celebrity circuit, you can generally assume that everyone knows everyone, at least at one stage removed. And it turned out we'd all met Jodie, who, while she can come across as a touch . . . brittle on camera, is a different proposition when you meet her in person, in, say, the VIP area of China White. Okay, she blanked me as usual, but she rushed up to hug a blushing LB, now back in his element as Donovan, meanwhile, performed the introductions, and Prescott just stared, at LB in particular, as if something in his world had gone horribly wrong.

'I'd didn't realise this was a bloody kids show,' he muttered.

Dinner was served in Jason's garden, the menu consisting of shrimps, on the barbie, steaks, on the barbie and, in what was to prove to be something of a theme that week, I can't remember what the dessert was.

Anyway, from the off it was clear that Prescott saw himself as a cut above the rest of us. Two G&T's in, and he was already starting.

'You see, when I was your age, I was a union man. Jobs, real life, that's what I was about. But you lot . . . you'd turn up for the opening of a bloody gas bill.'

'What's a gas bill?' said LB.

'I'm going to pretend I didn't hear that . . . let's take you as an example, Jason. I mean, the West End, it's all very fancy, but it's hardly work for a grown man, is it? Tell me, what do you think you've achieved?'

'Mate,' said Donovan, 'I don't mean to be rude, but what have *you* achieved? At least Andrew Lloyd Webber never invaded Iraq.'

'That's right,' said Jodie, who'd had a few Martinis, 'that war was illegal.'

'No it bloody wasn't. Everyone's a critic these days, but tell me this – is the world, or is the world not, a better place without Saddam Hussein?'

'What's a Sodom Hussein?' said LB.

'And as for you,' snapped Prescott, 'I have no *idea* what your claim to fame is.'

'That's Lavender Bunny,' said Jodie. 'He's a spokesman for his generation.'

'God help it then. A grown lad with a bloody teddy, it's pathetic.'

'I don't know if you can tell, Mr Prescott,' I said, 'but Lavender Bunny is giving you a hard stare.'

'Is he? Well, he can bugger off then. You tell him a few years in a factory would sort his ideas out. And yours.'

'He also wants to know if you bummed your sex-cetary.'

'Right. Stop filming.'

We were referred to a clause in our contract. Certain subjects, it transpired, were off limits. LB and I were taken aside by the show's director, but still, it took a while for Prescott to be coaxed back to the table. A bit of a diatribe about phone hacking followed. It turned out – when the others could get a word in edgeways – that everyone had been a victim.

'Yes, but it's not the same,' said Prescott. 'In my case, there were serious questions to do with national security!'

'But shouldn't you have kept in your trousers then, Prescott?' said LB.

'I *beg* your pardon? Kept *what* in my trousers?'

'I don't know. But that's what the papers say anyway.'

'I see. You read the papers, do you?'

'Yes. Don't you?'

'Have you been listening to nothing I've been saying? No, I bloody well do not!'

'Okay,' said Jason after an uncomfortable silence, 'I thought we could maybe play some charades?'

Next up was Jodie. In her charming Essex home, she cooked spring rolls, duck and . . . something or other. As with Jason, we scored her a seven. Jodie keeps an excellent cellar, but the atmosphere was a bit strained, particularly during the limbo dancing, LB and Prescott now visibly jostling for Alpha Male status, the former Deputy Prime Minister making various cracks about Keith Harris, and Orville, while LB, who'd done some research on my laptop, was full of questions about what 'Two Jags', 'Two Shags', and so on meant.

Day three. Prescott, in a grace-and-favour flat he'd borrowed for the evening, he said, served up what he described as 'good, old-fashioned home cooking', like his mother used to make, when his family had 'barely a pot to piss in'. So leek soup, I think, followed, contentiously, by rabbit stew.

'Prescott,' said LB, as the dish was served, 'can I go to

the toilet?'

'What?'

'He says he gets a bit nervous, using other people's bathrooms. He prefers to go al fresco.'

'And what's that supposed to mean?'

'Well Prescott,' said LB, 'if you've no outside loo, don't that make you a Tory?'

At this point, Prescott, never the least volatile of public figures, even while sober, grabbed LB by the scruff of his ears and whipped him over to the casserole, boiling on the stove.

'Mock my roots will you? You bloody little snob!'

'John mate,' said Jason, 'steady on there. You were pretty rude to Lavender Bunny.'

'I am not here to be insulted!'

'LB says . . .' I said.

'What? What does he say?' said Prescott. 'And how the bloody hell are you communicating with him anyway? Telepathy?'

'He *says*,' I continued, retrieving a somewhat bedraggled LB from the *jus*, 'that whatever the dessert's like, he's giving you *one* this evening.'

'What?'

'Like you used to do to your research assistants, he says.'

Day Four. In our somewhat ill-appointed Whitechapel flat, LB and I were serving up oysters, *filet mignon* and the most expensive champagne we could find in Costcutter, Tempers, understandably, were now running high.

'Michael,' began Prescott, before he'd even accepted a glass of Clicquot, 'I've been perplexed by your friend's behaviour this week. So I Googled you. This isn't about that review I wrote, is it? For that novel of yours? Because if it is, can I repeat, here on national television, that it was a bloody travesty?'

'You slagged off Mike's book, mate?' said Jason.

'Yes I did!' said Prescott. 'And I'd do it again in a heartbeat!'

'Yes, he did,' said LB. 'Him, Will Self and Janet Waterstones got me and Mike banned from Stringfellows.'

'I *thought* I hadn't seen you around,' said Jodie. 'So what happened? What did you do?'

'Shat on the carpets, I shouldn't wonder.' said Prescott.

'Is that why you left politics, Prescott?' said LB.

'Don't attack him again, mate,' said Jason, stepping in hurriedly, 'it's not a good look.'

'Yeah, chill out, guy. So come on Mike,' said Jodie, 'I'm dying to hear . . .'

So I explained about our exile from the VIP area.

'Christ,' said Jodie, 'that was quick.'

'Yes. Yes it was.'

'Hey, I've just had a brainwave! Maybe LB could come along with me sometime? In fact, why not tonight? Would you like that, LB?'

LB nodded so vigorously that I feared his little heart might burst. Since he'd begun talking to me, I'd always at least tacitly accepted the possibility that my relationship with LB was something I should, by rights, have possibly been speaking to a doctor about, but . . . was I wrong about that? Had he now attained independent consciousness? Had I been holding him back, all this time?

'I'll make it worth your while,' said Jodie, seductively twirling her golden extensions, 'when it comes to the scoring, Mike.'

'Interesting,' said Prescott. 'I assume the rabbit's plus one will *not* be attending?'

'Well, no. No offence Mike, but it might spoil the photo-ops.'

So that was three days ago. Apart from an appearance in the *Daily Star*'s gossip pages, I haven't seen LB since. I fear that fame, once again, with its intoxicating sweetness, may rather have gone to my young friend's head. Nor is Jodie returning my phone calls. Which leaves me here alone, pretty much, with a bottle of scotch. What am I going to write about now, without LB to inspire me? The Big Brother money won't last forever, so will I have to get back into gainful employment, after all this time? As situations go, I think I'd have to score this about a two out of ten.

Which, for what it's worth, was the mark Prescott gave my evening, thus ensuring that LB and I finished third. It's a source of comfort though, cold as it might be, that Prescott, as is often the case when contestants get violent, came last.

At the end of the show, though it was never actually broadcast, (for a peer of the realm, and a notorious brawler, the big man's surprisingly sensitive) LB said;

'Well done, Prescott. That must be a first, for you.'

Prescott hit him in the face.

MATT MITCHELL'S MURDEROUS MANIACS

About the first thing they tell you when you show up at drama school, and they don't let up much for the next three years, is that it doesn't really matter what it is, panto in the Falklands, some cunt out of film school's first, very personal feature, which usually involves you freezing your nuts off in a warehouse somewhere, covered in stage blood, screaming about your mum, or an ad campaign for a major high street bank, you should never say no to a bit of work. That actors act, they don't 'rest'. That what they specifically don't do is sit around in front of the afternoon racing, dreaming of glory at the RSC.

And it's not bad advice. But it's not great advice, either. Tom, a mate of mine from college, who'd played a blinder as Prospero at the end of our third year, got lamped in the pub the other week by some aspiring entrepreneur, or nutter, who'd just had a loan for his business rejected, and arrived in the boozer on the warpath. basically.

'I'm sorry to hear that,' Tom said, collared outside in a bar on the river, wearing a scarf – quite a posh lad is Tom, which may have inflamed the situation. 'But I'm a mere thespian.'

'You're a *what?*'

'I mean I'm an actor . . . I'm only an actor. I don't actually work there.'

'Oh yeah? You took their money though, didn't you?'

'But it was just for the day. And I'm not sure the ad was meant to be an accurate depiction of life at the bank . . . you don't seriously think they go around giving each other high five the whole time, do you?'

'Actually, yeah, I do.'

'You may have a point there . . . but shouldn't you be taking this up with your branch manager?'

'But I'm taking it up with you, you cunt.'

'And I'm telling you, mate, that I really can't help you. I wish I could, but honestly, I wouldn't know a fixed rate mortgage from a kick in the balls.'

Bad choice of words that, as it turned out.

'You have to pay your dues in this game, Matt.' said Tom over the dog from his hospital bed a few days later. 'You have to take a few lumps and I accept that. But not in the face, surely? I could have understood if I was a villain in a soap. But just for an advert?'

'Well, it is quite an annoying ad, mate. It's on all the time.'

'I know, I know. What a laugh we all have there, selling ISA's to an unsuspecting public . . . I can't even watch telly, Matt, in case the bloody thing comes on . . . what are we doing here? Where are the great roles? When will we ever play . . . the Dane?'

'Don't ask me, mate. Ask the agent.'

'Ah yes,' said Tom brightening slightly. 'How goes it with the tartan beast of NW2?'

'Fuck knows. I'm supposed to ring him. Apparently, there's some work on, but he doesn't say what.'

'He never quite does, does he?'

'No.'

'Oh well.'

'Oh well indeed, mate.'

'Yeah.'

So;

'Listen, McTavish . . . no, you listen mate,' I was saying to the agent, over the dog a few days later, 'Matt Mitchell is a trained, classical actor . . .'

'Now Matthew,' replied McTavish, in his sinister, creamy Morningside drone, 'dinnae be so melodramatic. Quite apart from anything else, I wonder you're established enough to refer to yourself in the third person?'

'And whose fault's that? You kilted bell-end?'

'I beg your pardon?'

So, matters between myself and McTavish had deteriorated lately. But no wonder, really. I, Matt Mitchell, who'd done Ibsen, who'd played Pinter, who'd graduated with honours from his class at drama school, had got off to a fairly promising start career-wise, starring as a hard-drinking, wife-beating teenage father in BBC3's surprise ratings smash, *Alcopop*, to some fairly decent notices.

'The Sick Face of Young Britain' the Sun had observed, if seemingly a bit unclear as to whether the film was a documentary or not. I steal the child benefit and spend it on crack. I dish out some shoeings left, right and centre, to any mother, young or otherwise, who tries it on. In the climactic scene, my character hits a Holland Park pre-natal class with a few cans of petrol, and beer.

'This is for all the geezers who don't wanna be trapped!' I shout. 'I did my best as a Dad!'

I go up in flames. Everybody goes up in flames.

Okay, it was BBC, council estate, lifestyle porn. Though I say so myself it was pretty good, but, had my performance been too convincing? Had I come across as too unlovable for mainstream telly? I was no oil painting, it's true, and in the reviews, there'd been a suggestion that I looked like nothing so much as a young Bob Hoskins, or worse still, Wayne Rooney. That is, just Wayne Rooney.

Not a younger version. Getting into the acting racket, that isn't the kind of thing you want to hear.

Anyway, for whatever reason, since *Alcopop*, the expected offers from the soaps had failed to materialise. At least unless you're including my West Ham Fan on *The Bill*, my Second Hoodie in a *Hollyoaks* special, and most recently, which says a fair bit about the direction my career was taking, my Dead Crack Dealer, in an unusually hard-edged edition of *Midsomer Murders*. So what it all boiled down to was basically this – was I now in danger of being type-cast, of being stuck in the same moody tracksuit and Arsenal top combo until I found myself literally driving a mini-cab? It was beginning to look like a real possibility.

So I'd taken the call from McTavish's office with a hangover, basically.

'Matthew,' he said, 'I understand your frustration. You are a serious artiste. Rome, however, wasnae built in a day.'

'Yeah, but how exactly is me giving another young mum a kicking on *Holby City* going to help with that, McTavish?'

'I can only work with the clay I've been given, Matthew. Now tell me, are you familiar with Danny Dyer, the actor? Star of *Human Traffic* and *The Football Factory*?'

'Are you mugging me off, mate? All I seem to be up for is parts that knobber's turned down.'

'I believe I have explained to you, Matthew, about the pecking order in these matters. The chain of command, as it were.'

'Yeah, yeah,' I said, reciting the mantra. 'There's Caine, Hoskins and Winstone, the premier league. Then Phil Daniels, Danny Dyer, the first division. And then Millwall. Crystal Palace . . . Leyton Orient . . .'

'The new breed, Matthew. The coming young things. Although there's rather a glut of you laddies at the moment, it's true.'

'That's supposed to make me feel better about what, exactly?'

'I am about to tell you, if you'll let me get a word in edgeways . . . now, young Dyer has recently been getting some *very* decent ratings – ratings, let me tell you, that were perhaps not expected – for his series on Bravo, *Danny Dyer's Deadliest Men.*'

'Yeah, I've seen it.'

'Really? That's marvellous. I'm afraid I haven't, myself.'

'Too busy having dinner at The Ivy, eh mate?'

'Don't be a bore, Matthew dear. Now, here's the situ . . .'

So the situ was this: In series one of his show, Dyer had interviewed a series of colourful characters, ex-football hooligans, ex-bare knuckle boxers, ex-armed robbers and so on. All now reformed, to be sure, but all still happy enough to take a walk down memory's back alleyways, for an appropriate fee. Well fair enough, I suppose. In crime, as on stage, you more or less have to make to make your own pension arrangements. And all this, as McTavish said, had been a bit of a hit. But in TV, as in crime, you can't rest on your laurels. So in series two, the stakes had been raised, as Dyer spent a few nights round the deadly men's houses, meeting their better halves, having dinner with the family and seeing how they lived. Invariably, he'd start off 'shitting himself' – and given the format, who could blame him – but they'd always ending up bonding down at the local, over a few pints.

So what the powers that be at Steve TV (it's low on the menu if you've got Sky or cable, but it is there) wanted to do was make a pilot for a similar, but edgier, and more youth-orientated show, in which *someone*, (i.e. muggins here), would take the *Deadly Men* concept to 'the next level'.

Which brings us back, pretty much, to where we came in.

'So basically, McTavish,' I said, after he'd laid out the scenario, in his usual uncertain terms, which had got bigger names than me into ads for cat food, breakfast cereal, and in one case, famously, for Toilet Duck, 'they want me to get off with the geezer's bird?'

'Always with the drama, Matthew . . .'

'Okay, to *try*, at least, to get off with not one, not two, but what is it, *six* of the better halves of men who have done, between them, about eighty years in prison? Do I sound, to you, McTavish, like I want to be part of the London Olympics?'

'I am encouraging all my clients, Matthew, to take an active interest in 2012.'

'I mean literally a part of it. Buried alive in the stadium, mate.'

'You don't think you're exaggerating slightly?'

'McTavish, just because it looks like I've done a stretch in borstal, it doesn't mean I'd last five minutes in there.'

'Now Matthew, I'm sure that's not true . . . certainly, it's hard to picture you encountering difficulties in the showers . . .'

'What's that supposed to mean?'

'Just my little joke, Matthew. Anyway, it's not your skills as a fighter that are required here, so much as your abilities as a lover.'

'Yeah well, one thing leads to the other, in my experience.'

'Exactly! And it's your experience we're after here, laddie. You know how to talk to these people.'

'Yeah, you say, "sorry sir, yes, I did spill your pint, I'll get you another one," and then you get out of Dodge for a couple of months. What you don't do is turn round and try and give the bloke's Doris the benefit.'

'Nobody's talking about giving anyone *the benefit* Matthew. Why, if that were true, you'd barely be more than a common ponce.'

'Yeah.'

'Look, you were not Steve TV's first choice, Matthew, it's true. They were after someone a wee bit more . . .

picturesque. But chin up! I gather they're fond of the old sobriquet.'

'The . . . what?'

'Your name, Matthew. The alliteration.'

'Yeah, I got that, McTavish. Alfie Allen turned this down right?'

'I gather young Allen was otherwise engaged, yes. But don't let that put you off.'

'No . . . so it's going to be called, what, *Matt Mitchell's Mobbed-Up Monsters*?'

'I don't think the interviewees would take too kindly to that description, do you?'

'*Matt Mitchell's Many Mentalists*?'

'Thankfully Matthew, your input on that level will not be required.'

'Wait, I know. *Matt Mitchell's Murderous Maniacs.*'

'Christ,' said McTavish, 'must I always be surrounded by silly wee laddies?'

'That's a question that'll have to be answer eventually, I suppose.'

'Oh shut up. Look, you're always complaining about not being stretched in your work. So you could think of this as an opportunity to show your range. To put your best foot forward as a mischievous, cockney, Jack the Lad sort. Everybody loves that rubbish, these days. Otherwise, of course, you're more than welcome to pursue an alternative career at the turf accountant's, Matthew, pickling your insides with drink and regrets.'

'So it's like that, is it? I've got big dreams, I want fame, but fame costs. And right here's where I start paying, in sweat?'

'That's very eloquently put. You young laddies, you come out of stage school with no bloody clue, expecting the world on a platter . . .'

'RADA, mate,' I said. 'I went to RADA. As I believe it says on my CV.'

'Oh aye, so it does. Still, no amount of college education is a substitute for paying one's dues. Why, I remember my own youth, touring the country in our trusty wee transit . . . experimental theatre, that was where it was at . . . it was a very different time.'

'Yeah, well, the less said about it the better. But what are you saying, that I haven't suffered enough for my art?'

'Your words, Matthew. Not mine.'

'But McTavish, 'I was about to ask him, 'how can you say that, when you've been my agent for the last four years?'

It was at this point, however, that McTavish quoted a figure.

'I see . . . straight up? Just for a pilot?'

'Indeed. And there would, of course, be more to follow, subject to a satisfactory performance.'

'Right.' I said. 'Right.'

If this sounds like an iffy idea for a TV series, then that's because it was. But it was never broadcast. Consider what does get shown, *Dogs With Jobs* and so on, and then imagine the projects that don't make the cut. Beneath what you see on telly, there is another, darker world.

And so it was that a few weeks later, I found myself outside a mock-Tudor mansion in darkest Basildon. It was ten in the morning, and I was making my way through a four-pack of Stella, the old wife-beater, ironically enough, I thought, as Clifton Styles, the subject, came pimp-rolling down his front drive. Should I, with hindsight, have started drinking so early? Well, probably not, is the answer to that, but it was strange to be back.

'Okay Matt,' said Seb, the director. 'Ready to roll, yes?'

'I feel like dropping the kids off, mate, as it goes.'

'Really?' said Seb, not inspiring much confidence in his understanding of the *milieu* we were about to enter. 'I didn't know you had children.'

'If this comes on top, mate,' I said, 'there's a fairly good chance I never will.'

The problems implicit in bonding with Styles, never mind his good lady, were clear from the outset. He was from round my area (I'm a Basildon boy myself, hence the move into acting, as soon as I could) but I'd never heard of this bloke. So in the van on the way over, I'd gone through his charge sheet. Which all seemed to date from a Tuesday morning back in the Nineties, when Styles, instead of watching Sky Sports or the Adult channel, had opted instead to pay a visit to his local Barclays, to discuss his account. Well, fair enough, you might think, except it's probably not if you've been up smoking crack for a couple of days, and if, what's more, you've forgotten to leave your Uzi at home. Going to the bank being a frustrating business at the best of times. To be fair to the bloke, he'd always claimed to regret this, but then you would do really, if, in the space of fifteen minutes, you'd pretty much scuppered your alleged drugs empire, and on top of that earned yourself ten years in Pentonville. Even with time off for good behaviour, or at least, for not getting done for any more bad behaviour, that was still an expensive morning's work. Probably best not to mention that, though.

So here he was now, the man of the hour, maybe five-six, five-seven, in shades, lots of gold and a white Prada tracksuit. With his shaved head and tatts, he looked like nothing so much as toddler with form, but always beware of the short man's issues, and that's especially true if there's a fairly good chance that he still has weapons stored in his home.

'Clifton mate,' I said, offering a hand, 'how you doing, bruv?'

'I ain't,' said Styles, 'your brother. You cunt.'

The morning sun flashed off his jewellery, the SUV parked in the driveway, and his wife's blonde extensions. His wife, that was, who was standing in the doorway like a fairytale princess, who'd been trapped in a castle by an evil dwarf . . . or conceivably just by an eye-popping boob job. What were they, double E? Double F? Whatever, it couldn't have been easy to get around Basildon with those on display. Maybe I could do this, after all?

'My apologies, Mr Styles.' I said. 'Thank you for inviting me . . . sorry *us*,' I went on, making a point of including the film crew, 'into your lovely home.'

'Yeah,' Styles said, 'fucking gorgeous, innit? See anything you like?'

'Well, I love with what you've done with the garden, mate.'

'Yeah. Are you looking at my wife?'

'Well . . .' I said, inwardly wishing a dose of clap on McTavish. This being the hard man's version of a zen koan. In that however you answer it, you're almost bound to get a slap.

'I said, are you looking at my wife?'

'I, err . . .'

'So you're saying she's a dog then?' said Styles.

'No, mate, what I'm saying is . . .'

'What? You ain't saying nothing, are you?' snapped Styles, before slinging a stubby arm over my shoulder, and adding, with a evil, gold-toothed grin, 'I'm only having a giggle. You look like you've done a shit in your knickers, mate.'

'Yeah, I had a few too many last night, as it goes . . .'

'What fists up your arse? Listen, Mitchell, or whatever your name is,' said Styles, the temperature, in spite of the sunshine, apparently dropping by quite a few notches, so much so that I suddenly did fear for the state of my boxers, as well as my teeth, fingers and so on – for a short bloke, he did have presence. 'Don't feel shy on my account. If you've got something you want to say, just spit it out.'

No, nothing, Mr Styles,' I said. 'Nothing.'

'Good,' said Styles, after an uncomfortable silence. 'Right then, let's crack on.'

The next problem with the shoot appeared to be this, that while some of Dyer's deadly men had presumably heard of, and maybe even seen a few of his films, it soon became clear that Styles had no real idea who Matt Mitchell was. That he was under the impression we were there from *Grand Designs*, or one of the other property porn shows.

Still, that wasn't a totally bad thing, I supposed, seeing as Debs, the long-suffering, while she obviously wasn't going to have much of a say in the slice of Marbella Styles was trying to create here, was still invited along on the tour of the estate. Of the projected summerhouse and the half-built pool, and the recently-completed Tudor-style villa. Which gave me the chance to put in some spadework, a quip here and there, the odd cheeky grin, before, after one too many questions about E's in the Nineties (extortion, Ecstasy, Essex, et cetera) the penny finally dropped.

A tricky few minutes then ensued. Clearly, I couldn't exactly tell Styles what we were really doing there, but I think I just about managed to smooth things over. At least, it appeared to be sufficient to the hour for everyone to accept that these days, Clifton Styles was a legitimate businessman. That Clifton Styles had always been a legitimate businessman, and that anyone who thought otherwise could meet him in the alleyway round the back of his local.

Which brought me to my next suggestion, that we visit the pub, for some local colour. And so it was that six hours later, as we came stumbling out of the Steve TV people-carrier, Styles singing *I'm Forever Blowing Bubbles*, before collapsing in the drive like a wounded animal, everything seemed to be going pretty swimmingly.

'Oh God,' Debs said, 'plastered again and it's not even seven . . . how d'you let him get like this?'

'Don't look at me, Mrs Styles,' I said. 'I wanted to stick

to the beers, as it goes. But he's a hard man to argue with.'

'Don't I know it . . . all right, let's get him inside . . . yeah, you lot and all,' Debs said to the film crew. 'And you can turn that bloody thing off too. I don't know what he's been saying, but if you even think about showing it, you'll be hearing from his brief . . . his brief if you're lucky.'

'Of course,' said Seb, looking pretty much traumatised, after the five solid hours of bloodcurdling anecdotes we'd just endured. Still, courage Matt, I was thinking. Strength. The show must go on.

Styles safely ensconced in the spare bedroom then, ('Let him sleep it off the filthy, drunken pig!') Debs insisted we stay for dinner.

'It's the least I can do', she said, as we sat down in the dining room, 'And I don't see many people, now the kids have grown up,' she went on, before adding, coyly, 'you wouldn't think it now, but I used to be an actress myself.'

'Oh nonsense, Mrs Styles,' I said, having wondered about this earlier, 'you're a very attractive lady.'

'Cheeky!' laughed Debs, Seb and the others just looking on, horrified. But perhaps the greatest compliment you can pay anyone who's starred on the stage or the silver screen, (and Caine, Hoskins and Dyer would agree, I'm sure), is that you've watched one of their performances all the way through, more than once. As, I explained to Mrs Styles, had been the young Matt's experience with *Essex Babes 11*.

'You remember that?' Debs said.

'Oh yeah. Vividly.'

'Now you, Mr Mitchell,' she said, her décolletage looming as she topped up my Chardonnay, 'can call me Debs.'

'And you,' I said, thinking, bingo, you rogue, 'can call me Matt.'

So the wine duly flowed, and the gin and the Malibu, along with tales of times past, of the glory days of late Eighties showbiz, when Debs, it turned out, had been to a lot of parties. And met a lot of the players, directors, producers, agents and so on, the stars of successful ITV dramas, in what apparently hadn't been more innocent times, after all. That world of Piat D'or, yachts and *Poison* perfume. And all this, she said, when she'd been a buxom ingénue (my words, not hers) of just eighteen.

'Or at least, Mr Mitchell . . .'

'Matt, please.'

'Oh yeah. Well anyway, that's what I'd say to get into the clubs.'

'Right. So then how did you get into modelling?'

'Well Matt, I was working as a receptionist at the time. But I hadn't really been hired for my secretarial skills, you know? So I thought I could stick around in the City until I got married, being eyed up by the blokes there all day anyway, or I could take arms against a sea of troubles, you know? I mean, everyone seemed to think of me naked anyway . . .'

'Really?' I coughed.

'Yeah . . . so moving into glamour work just seemed like the logical step. All I was doing was sitting there smiling. Why not do it with my clothes off? For about a third of the hours, and eight times the money?'

'I can't really argue with that.' I don't remember saying, but it's there on the tape, Debs having been persuaded, without too much trouble (she had the biz in her blood, after all, as well as three or four snowballs, by this point) to let us start filming again.

'I could see all that Greenham Common stuff going out the window, Matt. You know, everyone wanted to party again? All that about not wearing miniskirts – I just thought, who decides? Some mad old bint on a college course somewhere, or me?'

'Yeah,' I said. In a way, I was disengaged from Seb and the film crew. Being back in Basildon, once again drunk and enraptured by Debs, was a Proustian experience.

Twelve years earlier I'd been a big fan, and here I was now, on the other side of the mirror. By now, I'd had four bottles of Stella, plus another five or six pints, a couple of shots and a few glasses of wine. I felt indestructible.

'I mean I'd left school with an O level in art and a couple of CSE's, Matt,' Debs continued, 'but I didn't see the point of beating myself up about it.'

'I know what you mean.'

'It wasn't a hard decision. What was the difference between me and the girls doing Page 3? A boob job, a tan and a bit of luck?'

'Yeah. So you went up by . . . quite a few sizes, I'm guessing . . . well, we all have to pay our dues somehow, I suppose . . .'

'What are you on about, Matt? These?'

'I . . . yeah.'

'Oh come on, there's no need to be bashful Actually, shall I tell you who you remind me of?'

'Bob Hoskins?' I supposed. 'Wayne Rooney?'

'Now you mention it, there is a resemblance. But no, I was thinking more Benny Hill.'

'I see . . .'

'He was a lovely man, you know?'

'I'm sure he was a great man, Debs, but he must have been about sixty when you knew him . . . how can you possibly think that?'

'Oh, I don't know . . . I just do.'

'Seb,' I said, into the camera, 'we can edit this, right?'

'At this point Matt, what'd be the difference?'

'Good.' I said. 'So anyway Debs, about your career . . .'

'My boobs, yeah? Well, these are the upgrades. They came a bit later. They were a wedding present, actually.'

'Yeah,' I said. 'You seem a bit more . . . generously proportioned than I remember.'

(I know, I know, but what can I tell you? You can take the boy out of Basildon . . .)

'What, are you saying you don't like them?'

'Not at all, Mrs Styles. Not at all. Anyway,' I went on, 'where were we . . .'

If anything though, Debs' anecdotes turned out to be even less suitable for telly than her husband's had been. While Styles had subtly, and then not so subtly, alluded to a series of events to do with, among other things, certain night clubs, pubs and new-build properties in Nineties Essex, at least most of the faces he'd mentioned weren't really in a position to take legal action. For just the reasons you'd think But this wasn't the case with a lot of the names Debs had met on her travels through London's hot spots, during much the same period From what I could gather, if we'd thought about trying to show any of that, Steve TV legal would have had kittens, a fit.

By rights then, we should have left it there. We should have packed up the cameras and gone back to London, for an almost certain bollocking from the show's producers, to maybe try and reschedule for another occasion, when everyone involved wasn't quite so sloshed.

But I must have been starstruck by Debs' showbiz memories. And so decided that while this wasn't exactly King Lear at the Royal Vic, I was still a professional, and had to at least have a go at the money shot, or risk losing my fee for the pilot altogether. So I rallied my strength and I rallied my training. I rallied the dregs of the Mitchell charm, and suggested something on the lines of a quick, cheeky snog, like an autograph, I said, for old times' sake.

I've had better ideas, though. As might have been predicted, given the way the shoot had gone so far (but you never see this sort of thing coming, until it's too late) there was a thump on the stairs, and a roar by the doorway, and the Clifton Styles, mock-Tudor, Spanish villa-type dining room went a bad shade of black.

So, what's to be said, now I'm here in the trauma ward,

where I'll be for a bit?

Well, that Clifton's lawyers and Steve TV legal appear to have come to a compromise, and that I won't be selling my story to the tabloids, after all. That the footage, while it is pretty interesting, like early Scorsese meets *Celebrity Wife Swap*, will probably never be shown, at least outside of the confines of a couple of private, Soho screening rooms. And that once I get out of hospital, I could easily end up back on the set of *The Hospital*, or *Holby City*, ironically enough. But that it's hard to feel totally negative about the whole situation. Because for one thing, being saved, as I was, by the lovely Debs is a memory I'll treasure (or at least, it's a memory I *would* treasure anyway – again, all I have is a tape) and for another, I must, after the hiding I took, be pretty much stuffed as a TV hard man.

If Bob Hoskins, say, had, at the start of his career, been kicked in on camera by a short-arse like Styles, and then into the bargain been rescued by his lady, of all people, it's difficult to see how his standing in the business would have recovered. No more roles as a gangster for 'Oskins. No *Long Good Friday*, no *Mona Lisa* ... actually, looking at it that way, what did I do?

Still, courage, Matt. Strength. Remember your training. Remember Daniels, Dyer and the rest of the blokes. Remember where the painkillers are.

Phew.

So being a geezer on screen is an act, of course. But the way the telly is these days, if you can't keep it up you're in bother, it seems. It's all about front, it's about self-respect. That I've now been outed as having not much of either arguably isn't so good – I'll maybe know more once McTavish gets in touch, which, needless to add, he hasn't done so far, the iffy Scotch git. But still, bandaged up here, with all this chirping machinery, on what really does feel like a career-changing path I suppose I'll be put forward for different roles, from now on. Whether the floppy-haired students, background accountants and expendable best friends I should think I'll be playing from now on will lead me any closer to my dreams of glory at the RSC remains to be seen. But it has to be a step in the right direction.

If nothing else, surely no one can now say I haven't paid my dues? Or that I have not suffered enough, for my art?

I've got a bad feeling about this, to be honest.

SARAH PALIN'S YULETIDE EPISTLE 2009

Hey y'all!

It's that time again! Christmas greetings from the Palins, here in sunny Alaska!

It has been an eventful year for the Palin family. You know us, never a dull moment! But where to begin? With the man of the house, I reckon.

Contrary to what you may have read, Todd has been *working all the hours God sends* with his business. With a li'l ole off-shore drilling project he's been putting together. Those pesky, out of state environmentalist types may not understand what Todd and the boys from BP are trying to achieve here, but we still believe in progress, here in Alaska. We believe in Big Oil, no one more than Todd, who at the end of a long day out on the ice fields simply does not have the time or the energy for any of the leisure time activities he has been accused of pursuing in the liberal press. Hell, the way we get written about, y'all would think it was like the last days of Rome, up here in Alaska! Nothing could be further from the truth. The only wild-catting Todd has been doing is for the good of this state, and this great nation of ours!

Meantime, I am now a grandmother. Grandma Sarah

. . . I can't believe it sometimes. Seems like only yesterday I was sitting under the bleachers, drinking a beer, riding around in a truck, being crazy . . . perhaps as a result of related behaviour, then, (though she was always a tad too feisty for her own good) Bristol, my eldest, has given birth to a bouncing baby gal. Out of wedlock, as y'all may have gathered from the muck-raking 'newspaper' reports, but I expect that situation to change very shortly. That young man will be walked up the aisle and into the ministry of Jesus with a goddamn AK-47 if necessary, Todd says. That husband of mine. He has such a way about him.

As for the youngsters, Piper, Willow and Trig (sometimes I wonder how Todd and I ever thought of those names!) they are walking righteously in the eyes of the Lord. Or at least Trig is not, yet. Todd already reckons he'll make a fine soldier, and killer of moose and whatnot. He can see it in his eyes, he says, as he lies in his crib. Trig that is, not Todd!

Finally, Track, my eldest boy, arrived back home from Iraq in the fall, as a decorated veteran, I am proud to say. He used to remark, in his e-mails, that any damn fool (not exactly the words he used) could earn a Purple Heart, that 'all you have to do is show up and get shot, Ma'. But now he owns one himself, I am sure he feels differently. Not that he says very much on the subject. That, or any other. Too busy out all hours in his old haunts, I reckon. He likes to spend a lot of time in the woods, with his rifle and hunting knives. I reckon the critter population's taken a regular hiding since he returned! At least I think that's what he's been doing. Still, while I do not agree with some of his recent 'fashion decisions', with the black trenchcoat in particular.

'Track', I say to him, 'I know it must seem cold here after Iraq, but what's wrong with a fleece jacket? Just because we can see the Russians from here, it don't mean you have to dress like one, my friend.' However, he has served his country.

And if sometimes, I hear him screaming in the night, hollering up at that old Alaskan moon, well boys will be boys. He always did like to get his poor mother's goat, did Track. As y'all may know, we have butted heads on a number of occasions. And I am quite sure this new phase, the mood-swings, the English rock band t-shirts (in Alaska, 'English' means something different from what I guess it does in England, otherwise how would those guys even have a birth-rate?) is just that, a phase.

Track will be applying to a series of good Christian colleges in the new year, regardless. None of that 'Gulf War syndrome' bull-manure for him. I see him as . . . well, possibly not a doctor.

Which brings us on to li'l old me. Well, since the sorry events of November 2008 – it's not just myself I weep for, it's America – Sarah Palin has been far from idle. There have been my duties as governor of this great state of course, but I have also embarked on a very personal project, which has helped me to come to terms with what happened at the last election. Because you know me, this Alaskan gal don't like to be beat! And in particular not by a . . . *n*abob, a *n*arcissist, like our friend Mr Obama. It's a crying shame that a man like that can end up in the White House, in this country of ours. I think y'all know what I'm saying.

I will admit, then, that there were some black days after the election. I sometimes wondered if it had all been my fault. He was a panty-waist, granted, and not a well man, but had old Sarah's earthy, down-home approach to world events in some way contributed to Senator McCain's fall? For a while, I felt like maybe it had done. Some of the things they were saying in the media, about old Sarah trying to ban all those books from Alaska's libraries, or to get that man locked up for divorcing her sister . . . well they hurt, they did. To be clear, the only library in Alaska I'd ban, if I could, is Track's, but I am unable to even do that, to keep filth like *Ulysses* and *The Origin of Species* out of my own home, owing to the Yale lock Track's put on his door. I swear, that boy could barely hold a hammer straight before he was in the service! However, I digress.

The point is that all the dirt the Democrats slung at me, in their sleazy campaign, very different from the G.O.P's . . . well, some of it stuck. The suggestion that old Sarah really was as dumb as a moose's dingus . . . at times, my friends, I had doubts. It was a testing period.

And it all came to a head one evening when I was reading an e-mail that Track had sent me, from Iraq. With hindsight, my stance on the war was not one he shared, but I did not realise this at the time. So when he told me that all the boys in his unit were checking out a website called 'Sarah Palin – Hardcore' I took that as a gesture of solidarity. Well who wouldn't? In fact my heart swelled with pride when, at Track's suggestion, and in a spare moment after the election (I'd been far too busy on the campaign trail before) I Googled it.

The first thing I saw was an image of a lady who looked very like me, who had the same, dare I say, iconic, ponytail, designer frames and business suit look. With a black man's . . . appendage, his 'schlong', I believe is the technical term, inserted, how can I put this, where the Lord did not intend. Well so far so satirical, I figured. I had become used to people goofing on this kind of stuff during the election, so I wasn't shocked. I would have chosen the Statue of Liberty as a more appropriate image, I remember thinking, instead of old Sarah, but the message about the likely fate of this country under Obama was, while distastefully put, still appreciated.

Or so I thought. Upon further investigation, however, it proved to be . . . not that kind of website, at all.

Do you know what a 'spit-roast' is? Not a pot-roast – we've all had one of those, I'm sure! A spit-roast, however, is quite different. By the same token, it's one thing to learn what a MILF is, and quite another again to discover that in the eyes of some very sick individuals, you are one.

What had happened, it transpired, was that a group of the kind of people that the Lord struck down in Gomorrah (and yes, they were that, literally – really, I felt for her – I mean it has to hurt, right? Perhaps some of you know?) had dressed some gal off the streets up like yours truly, and then put her through what seemed like an exhaustive, and frankly eye-watering list of . . . unchristian activities. On the world-wide web, yet. I had thought that tramp Tina Fey was bad enough, riding on my coat-tails to fame with her 'comedy' routine. But this woman, this 'porn star', I guess you'd call her, was heading into perdition on the back of something, actually a series of somethings, that were far worse.

Should I rehearse what my lookalike, my 'insatiable' avatar, did on that website? There's every reason why not, but then again, I am a Republican. Explaining . . . uncomfortable truths is all in a day's work.

So there were . . . encounters between my doppelganger and an obviously very troubled blonde, who was standing in for Hillary Clinton. Well, points for casting I guess. She, 'I', and 'Condy Rice' were required to get some legislation onto the statute books, by any, and I mean *any*, means necessary. This involved 'meetings' with President Bushes senior and junior, Mr Obama, as discussed, 'Slick Willy' Clinton, Mrs Nancy Reagan and bizarrely, even in this context, all the great Republican heroes of Mount Rushmore. (I am unsure of names, but they *were* all Republicans, right? Otherwise I'd feel doubly violated). Anyway, it was not, it appeared an easy bill to get through congress. There was much play on the word 'congress' incidentally. They must have thought they were real bright, the people behind this. Probably, they went to Berkeley. The scene involving the pitbull in lipstick would tend to suggest that, certainly. However, I am simply not going there.

In any event, long story short, I was so exercised by all this depravity, that, paradoxically, it inspired me. Because I realised that if nobody else – certainly not that *nit*wit Mr Obama – was going to drag this country out of the cesspit into which it had flung itself, then Sarah Palin would just have to step up to the plate.

I had lost my innocence about certain matters, it's true, but I had found something much more valuable: a cause. A crusade, if you like. Sure, I felt bad for the protagonist of *Nailin' Palin*, but I felt worse for the kids who might accidentally stumble across this filth whilst Googling 'dogs do the funniest things'. Or related. It's about time this country learned that freedom of speech is a privilege, not a right. And as we all know – especially my husband Todd – privileges can be withdrawn.

So if this seems like an unfestive story, well hell no, Satan! Because this hockey mom is gonna clean house! You heard it here first, folks – Sarah Palin will run on a platform of purity in 2012! And in this season of goodwill and giving, I'm sure y'all will be glad to know that you can send your campaign donations to the usual address. Or simply log onto my new website! The tools of mine enemy shall be used against him, saith the Lord! I'm sure he said that somewhere. Although obviously, be careful 'on-line'.

Anyhoo, if you're still unsure about opening your checkbook, just ask yourself this: what's the most important gift you can give your children this Christmas – an iPod, or innocence – and I trust you'll find there's a book that matters more. The Good Book!

With best wishes for a happy, and prosperous, New

Year for you and your family.
Praise the Lord, and pass the ammunition!
Sincerely,
Your friend (and Jesus's)!

Sarah Palin.

THE DISASTERS

Before the video shoot started, we were interviewed by the NME. Or at least, I was. Basil, perhaps distracted by the unusually high amount of Ex-Lax in his opiates (what sort of philistine could have done that to the spokesman for a generation?) spent most of it in the Gents, from where he had to be more or less stretchered for the photo session afterwards. Did I feel responsible, as Paul and Terry, the ex-special forces guys we'd had to hire to look after him, escorted Basil to the stage? I suppose I should have done. But I'd been trying to explain about the new album, about its themes and its influences, without being sure if anyone was listening. The focus, as ever, was on The Dying Boy.

'I'm sorry abut this,' I said to Emma, the journalist, while Basil was propped up just about long enough for one more iconic, Shane McGowan meets Keith Richards image to be captured on film. 'The, ah, food in Thailand didn't agree with him.'

'Right. But I thought he was a vegetarian?'

'Well, we all were. Vegans, pacifists, committed anti-capitalists . . . but what can I tell you? It was a long tour.'

'You see, I'd really like to talk to Baz about that. About where his head's at these days.'

'Yeah.' I supposed, looking round at the pub, at the cheap, hired instruments set up on the stage, at the glittering curtain that served as a backdrop, and the various extras arranged round the tables, dressed up as guests at a particular type of North London, religious ceremony. Was this a good idea? It was difficult to say. On top of our finances, our management and our image in the press, basically all the stuff you're supposed to think about, our moral compass had lately been in disrepair.

'I'm sorry, is there a problem?' said Emma, pushing her hair back, and her Wonderbra up, the music press having long since worked out that if they sent someone foxy to do the interviews then the bands, fools as we generally are, would be much more likely to open up, share, or otherwise spill out over the sides about all our issues. Certainly, I'd been flirting with her throughout, at least until I'd realised that as far as she was concerned, I was just the guitarist. 'Look, I understand if he's busy, but it would be great if I could have a couple of minutes with him, all the same.'

'I'm not sure that's going to be possible,' I said, as Basil fell off the makeshift crucifix he'd been posing for the photos on, and then, heroically I suppose, righted himself, and made his way to the bar at the back of the room. 'He needs his space before a performance.'

'Sure,' said Emma, tracking Basil's progress as, oblivious to the film crew, he made his way through the lights and the cameras, with the lackadaisical air of a three day drunk in a glass museum. Even now, after all this time, his powers of recovery were still a source of amazement.

'But he looks all right to me.'

'Really?'

'Okay, not really. But if I could have maybe half an hour with him, you'd be guaranteed the front cover. Otherwise, I can't make any promises.'

'I see. But I think I've explained about the album . . .'

'Yeah, but speaking as a fan, not just a journalist, I'd like to talk to him about his lyrics. They're so poetic, you know? They really spoke to me.'

'Did they.' I muttered, into my lager.

'Yeah, they did. Listen, I don't know why you're being so difficult about this. Maybe I should have a word with your manager?'

'But Emma, I *am* our manager . . .'

'Really? I thought you guys were with Ted Mann?'

'No. It's a temporary situation, I'm sure, but we're in a . . . period of transition with that sort of thing, at the moment.'

'I see . . . that can't be easy.'

'No. But I try not to sweat the small stuff, you know?' I said, with what I thought was a raffish, devil-may-care smile, until I caught sight of it, reflected in the window. Sweating the small stuff, and the big stuff, and just the stuff in general looked to something I'd spent a lot of time doing. How had I let things get so out of hand?

'That's great. All right, cards on the table. If you want the cover,' said Emma, 'I'm going to have to insist.'

'What, on talking to Basil?'

'Who else?'

'Right. It's like that, is it?'

'I'm all over how like that it is.'

'Okay then.' I supposed, now seriously beginning to regret inviting her. Since when had the papers got so pushy? Had The Doors had to put up with this kind of treatment? Had Joy Division? 'But don't say I didn't warn you.'

'I think I can handle him.' said Emma. What was she, twenty one, twenty two, fresh out of college and still young and in love with the magic of rock and roll . . . she really was very beautiful. 'I've interviewed Pete Doherty, you know.'

'Really? How is Pete?'

'He's . . . fine, I guess. You know Pete.'

'Yeah. Good. But think of that as a small town,' I figured, staring hard at my beer, 'and now you're in the big city.'

'As I said, mate, I'm sure I can manage.'

'All righty . . . oh Basil dear,' I said, to the apparition by the optics, still facing away from us, so all we could see was his dyed silver crewcut, his frayed leather jeans, and the dragon tattoo that was crawling out of the sleeve of his Dire Straits t-shirt, and down past the marks in the crook of his elbow, a fanged head inked on the back of his hand. Not especially easy to get that through customs, which I suppose had been his point. 'Would you like to talk to the nice lady from the music papers?'

'No,' Basil said, in a faux-yardie accent that was no less grating for being recently acquired. 'And it's Baz, all right? You cunt.'

So, suburban dreams of stardom had come to this. I'd hoped we were going to be like Jagger and Richards, or Morrissey and Marr, and now it looked like we were. Bitter old queens at twenty five. I remembered thinking we could change the world. But if in our own small way we had, it seemed to have been mainly for the worse. Quite a few of the kids, if our website was anything to go by, had been inspired to go on marches, thanks to us. But I'd yet to read about anyone who'd taken up medicine or the law. Which, considering the amount of time we spent trying to stay out of court and A&E seemed unfortunate. Still, I wasn't inclined to let the ship go down just yet, even though in many ways, it was holed on all sides.

'Are there . . . issues?' wondered Emma, not unflirtatiously.

'No, I ain't got no fucking issues,' said Basil, now turning to face us, leaning round, his eyes so bloodshot, and so heavily kohled as to resemble a couple of bad stains on a hospital bed sheet. '*He's* the one with the fucking issues. I saw you sneaking off to the bogs earlier, mate.

Doing a cheeky bitta nosebag, were we?'

'No, mate,' I said, not entirely truthfully, 'I just went for a slash.'

'Oh yeah?'

'Yeah. Just because you can no longer use the Gents in the way God intended, doesn't mean everyone's in the same position.' I nearly replied, before biting my tongue. There had been rumours in the press about tensions in the band, plus crystal meth, Latvian porn stars and the terrors of the dragon, but so far, nothing had been confirmed. And it seemed for the best if we kept it that way. We weren't quite ready for the Priory album, so –

'Oh nothing,' I said.

'Right then, so shut it. Mate.'

'Okay, then everybody,' said Seb, the director. 'Are we ready to roll?'

'Five minutes?' I said.

'Well yes, all right, but we are on a clock here.'

'Understood . . . Basil, can we get on with this now?'

'Can we bollocks.'

'Look, we've been over this. It's not selling out if it's a product you'd buy anyway. And let's face it, mate, you're not averse to the occasional pint of vodka. So I don't know what what you're worried about.'

'You do what you want, mate, but I ain't no whore for the multinationals.'

'Right,' I said. 'Well, apart from the fact that we're on EMI, what else d'you think you look like, if it's not a rent boy?'

'This,' Basil said, as he stood up, kicked over his chair with a surprisingly well-aimed combat boot and went storming off back to the facilities, 'is why I'm fucking going solo.'

'He probably isn't going to do that.' I said to Emma.

'No? But what would you do if he did?' she said, suddenly, breathtakingly, interested, perhaps sensing a scoop.

'It's more a question of what he'd do, I think. Not that anyone's considered it, you understand ... anyway, I'd better get on.'

'Sure. I might stick around for the filming though, if that's okay?'

'Yeah, why not? What's the worst that could happen?'

So we'd been in the pub for a couple of hours by now, and it's fair to say tempers were beginning to fray. Sponsored, for reasons I'll get to, by a major drinks company, we were here to shoot the promo video for our new single *We Deserve It*, the first from our second album, *Dad, I'm Sorry*. It was your basic 'band crashes the wedding' scenario, with a twist. The guests, went the concept, who were OAP's from casting central, in costume as leading members of the North London Jewish community, doctors, lawyers, rabbis and so forth, are sitting around at a low-key reception, They are, the viewer's given to understand, a bot bored by the couple. She's an accountant, he's a dentist, they've seen it all before. And then we, the band, storm in off the street, grab hold of the instruments and kick out the jams, basically, turning the room into rock and roll Valhalla, the maddened pensioners rising out of their chairs and trance-dancing along, deranged in the strobe lights, before attacking the stage in a bacchanalian frenzy, and crucifying Basil in the final shot. Well, I know, but it was supposed to be ironic, or post-ironic, or possibly even post, post-ironic, or something like that. Plus, you need to make an impression on YouTube these days.

Anyway, joining us on set, along with Emma and the photographer, was Ian from the drinks company, a big fan of the band, he said, from way back. To begin with he'd been fine, quite 'hey guys, well met', but as the time had worn on he'd begun to look worried, with the air of a schoolboy on a trip to an abattoir, who's just had his first look behind the curtain, at where the magic really comes from.

'This is going to be okay, isn't it?'

'Well, Basil's very sensitive.' I said, refreshing our glasses. 'He's a complicated guy. It's not for me to say he's a spokesman for the u, of course, but whatever he is, it doesn't come in an easy package.'

'Understood,' said Ian. 'And the new album is great. The lyrics especially . . . Baz really seems to have matured as a songwriter.'

'Yes,' I said, through gritted teeth, fiddling with one of my skull rings, 'I think he surprised himself with a few of those.'

'Indeed. It's just . . . there isn't going to be a problem, is there? I mean we wanted something edgy, and we do understand that it's important for you guys to cultivate a rock and roll image . . .'

'Cultivate. Yes.'

'But,' Ian continued, suddenly steelier, no longer the buttoned-down suit-jockey I'd originally taken him for – it's a poor thing to be so judgmental, but you get nowhere in rock if you don't have an opinion, usually negative, about virtually everyone, 'you are going to be able to keep . . . the guys under control, right? Because it's a deal-breaker, I'm afraid, if Baz doesn't perform.'

'That should be all right'

'What,' shouted Basil from across floor, 'be the white man chatting 'bout now?'

'The price of your soul, Miss Drama.'

'Fuck off.'

'Okay then,' said Ian, 'I guess I'll leave you guys to it. It's just, one last thing . . . as a fan, you know, I was hoping to meet the rest of the band . . .'

'I understand. Bambi?' I said, addressing our stylish Japanese bassist, the heroine of over twenty thousand lurid fantasies, if her following on Twitter was anything to go by (why didn't I have twenty thousand followers on Twitter?)

who was dozing on the sofa next to us, and clad head to toe in sheer black leather. 'This is Ian.'

'Hi there Ian,' said Bambi, waking up briefly. 'Are you a bad boy? You look like a bad boy . . .' she continued, drowsily, 'you look like you need discipline.'

'I'm a married man . . .' said Ian. 'Oh God.'

Not for the first time, as Bambi went back to sleep, I wondered about what, as the guitarist, songwriter and latterly manager of this band, we'd all become.

So we were The Disasters, and that, pretty much, was how we lived. Officially influenced by no one at all, but in practice by Led Zep, The Doors and The Rolling Stones, in fact pretty much everyone who'd mislaid a key band member in unfortunate circumstances (Joy Division, Nirvana, The Sex Pistols – it's a hazardous profession) we had somehow, for reasons I'm still not sure I entirely understand, broken out of the toilet circuit a year or so earlier. To find ourselves with a top ten album right across Europe, an NME front cover (Basil in the foreground, the rest of us leaning against a wall behind him, slightly out of focus – it's an image I'm hoping our biographers will ignore) and a world tour to contend with. On the one hand it's great – You've got a voice, you're on television, you get paid, at least in theory, to travel the world by your adoring public, with sex, drugs and cocktails on tap for free. But it isn't always a recipe for success. If your singer's hell-bent on destroying your equipment, and as much of the stage as he can possibly get through on every single night of your first major trip round the British Isles, the expenses can start to ramp up dramatically.

So I'll never forget that fateful meeting with Ted Mann, of Mann Management, a few days after our triumphant performance at the Brixton Academy, when he showed me the tour accounts.

'We've made *a loss*?' I said.

'Yes, my brother,' Mann grunted, before sweeping a few

strands of thin, lank hair out of the way of his aviator glasses, and then applying himself to a stiff line of powder, racked up on a gold disc he'd taken off the wall. You hear a lot, these days, about cleaned-up record companies, and a more professional industry. About how it isn't the Nineties any more, and how if anyone's up at dawn these days, it's to go out jogging, or attend to the kids. And maybe that's true, most of the time. Some aspects of the biz, however, are still reassuringly old school.

'You want some of this?'

'No, you're okay. I'll have a scotch if you've got one, though,' I said, before adding, in what was to be the first in a series of ill-considered business decisions, 'Ted, we're probably going to have to sack you for this.'

'Excellent!' he chortled, the old horror. 'Well, my lawyers will be in touch!'

'Lawyers?' I cringed. 'But who's going to pay for that?'

'Oh, your label, I should think.'

'Really?'

'No mate, not really. It'll have to come out of your advance, I reckon.'

'Oh. Oh shit.'

'Spunked it all already, eh?'

'We've spunked it, Ted, on people like you.'

'Yeah well, welcome to the business, boy. It's all part of the game.'

'But we didn't sign up for any of this . . . well, okay we did, but weren't you supposed to look after us?' Just a little bit?'

'And that's exactly what I did, mate,' Ted chuckled. 'I looked after you, just a little bit.'

'Good one,' I sighed, still weak from the tour – all I'd eaten for a month was Ginsters pasties and LSD, it seemed. Mainly LSD. 'But is this really how you see your role in the industry?'

'I endure, son. That's all there is to it. I was in a band

myself once, you know.'

'Really?' I said, having heard about this a few times before.

'Oh yeah,' Ted said. 'We had the rave reviews, the lot. Until one day I asked myself; Ted, is eight stars out of ten and a NME front cover gonna get you the lifestyle you deserve? The place in the Cotswolds, the Ibizan villa, the five up, four down in Holland Park? The ex-model wife and the birds on the side? No Ted, I concluded, it wasn't.'

'I hadn't thought about it that way.'

'Yeah well, you should. Look at my office. Really look around.'

And it was opulent certainly, a vision in white, white walls, white ceiling, white deep pile carpeting, and a fair bit larger than most people's flats. The Damian Hirsts could have been fakes (with his spot paintings, it's often difficult to tell) but there was no doubting the quality of the view out the window, or the wide screen TV, or, given the way the Mann was sweating, the stuff racked up on his marble-topped work desk.

'Pretty nice, innit?'

'I suppose . . .'

'You *suppose?* Son, I like you, so I'm going to give you some good advice. Look at this lot,' he said, passing over the gold disc, a light dusting of powder falling onto the table. 'You've heard of them, right?'

'I have, yeah. Good band . . . Oasis before Oasis, almost. Nasty break-up though, wasn't it?'

'Well, the singer was a wanker. Actually they all were, apart from the guitarist. Who was a bloody genius.'

'Yeah.'

'And shall I tell you what the rest of them are up to now?'

'Playing the festivals? With somebody new on guitar, I suppose.'

'Exactly. Tell me, do you wanna be doing that when

you're in your mid-forties?'

'Well, it beats working in an office.'

'An office like this one? Have you seen my receptionist? Do me a favour.'

Chest heaving, Ted at this point seemed to drift into a reverie. Was he about to have a seizure? Hopefully not – it would have been a drag to have to speak to the police, never mind at Ted's funeral, as the last of his clients to see him alive. So;

'Ted,' I said, 'mate, I think there might be a problem with the record company.'

At this, the great beast snapped back to life.

'Tell them to fuck themselves,' he barked, eyes unglazing, swimming back into focus. 'Oh right,' he went on, 'sorry son, I was in world of my own there. What's the problem with the record company?'.

'Well, Basil showed up there with a paint gun the other day.'

'Right . . . doing a Stone Roses, was he? You wanna nip that in the bud.'

'I don't know if I can control him though, Ted.'

'Look son, take a tip from me. Just make sure you keep control of the publishing. Everything else is just details.'

These seemed like wise words. As did;

'Anyway, that concludes our business, I think. So are you sure I can't tempt you? This is primo nosebag, boy. Straight outta Bolivia.'

'I suppose,' I said, perhaps now sensing, for the first time, the way things were going to go, as Ted passed over the rolled-up note, 'that the sun has passed the yardarm.'

'Yeah. Running your own business, son, there's nothing like it.'

'Mm.'

'Anyway how's the gear? A bit stronger than what you're used to, eh?'

'Yeah . . .' I said, feeling as if, like Frankenstein's

monster, I'd just been electrocuted. This was, as Ted said, quite a lot stronger than what I was used to.

'There you go, son,' said Ted, patting me on the shoulder. 'You'll do, I reckon.'

'I feel like I'm having a heart attack, Ted.'

'But in a good way?'

'I . . . yeah. Well, this has been a great meeting . . . it's been a really great meeting, . . . but I've got loads of things I should be getting on with . . .'

'Oh bollocks, son. You're still officially under Mann Management's wing. The least we can do is give you a decent send off . . . Svetlyana,' he shouted, into the intercom, 'get your glad rags on, and book us a table, we're hitting the town!'

'But Edward,' replied the soft, husky voice, 'it is only Tuesday. You told me I must stop you from doing this until Thursday?'

'Yeah, yeah, but I'm trying to tutor this lad . . . if he's lucky, I might even manage him when he goes solo . . . now, where d'you fancy, son? The Ivy? One of Ramsays?'

'I'm not sure I could eat anything at the moment.'

'Yeah, I better hadn't, either. Watching the old waistline, and that . . . all right then, the boozer it is!'

'Oh Edward . . .' sighed the soft, husky voice.

Much, much later, after a series of cocktail bars, members only drinking clubs, and private dances in the VIP section of Spearmint Rhino, plus what may have been an interlude in some sort of high end bordello, or opium den, I woke up fully-clothed on the bathroom floor, feeling distinctly under the weather. Should I have listened to everyone, and become an accountant? I'd have been qualified by now, maybe even married. Car in the drive, nice place in the suburbs, would it have been so bad? Little Daniel and Jezebel heading off to the nursery, while the therapy dog ran around in the garden . . . it was a slow crawl back towards consciousness, standing up in itself no easy task, the room whiting out a couple of times before I got it together to look through my pockets, searching for clues, like the CSI guy at some kind of crime scene, where I was also the victim. Buried under the loose change, the crushed cigarettes and general detritus there was a note which read;

'Top evening! Here, as requested, is the geezer's number. Just remember not to ring him all the time. Everything in moderation, son! Ted.'

'No worries there . . .' I said, looking into the into the mirror. Looking at, what, a fairly run of the mill indie kid. With a rope of blood dripping out of his nose, its true, but still . . . how honest could I be about anything? So I made the call.

'Hey man . . . I'm, ah, Ted's friend? From last night?'

'Ah yes. He said you might be in touch. How're you doing, laddie?'

'I'm feeling like a blues musician, who's about to get shot. Honestly, I'd welcome the bullets.'

'I see. Well, that's easily fixed. Would you like a pick-me-up?'

'Probably . . . not that, no.'

'Something more soothing then? I may have just the thing.'

You could probably consider these famous last words.

Anyway, off we went, to tour the world. This is Basil on vocals, me on guitar, Bambi on bass and Dave on drums. Dave liked his ale, Bambi was into fashion, and if I was political, it was in only the loosest sense. Good things, not bad things. Save the Panda and so on. But it didn't much matter what the rest of us thought. As we made our way through Europe's fleshpots, Paris, Berlin and Amsterdam, for the first time traveling in a comfortable tour bus, Basil had plenty of time to catch up on his reading.

To be fair, there's history for this. We weren't the first

rock and rollers to express an interest in the aesthetics, at least, of Nazi Germany. David Bowie, Motörhead, they'd all dabbled. Our grandfathers had been executed largely because of the general question, that whole thing, but the chances were they wouldn't have liked us much, if they'd lived. They'd have thought we were bad Jews.

And they were great uniforms. And it was the first multinational. And who wouldn't, let's face it, hire Albert Speer as a set designer? Still, Basil's interest in the films of Leni Riefenstahl, The Protocols of The Elders Of Zion, and some of the more extreme ideas about the Jewish question available on the internet, began to seem worrying, after a while.

'Basil,' I'd say, 'we can't write an album about that.'

'Why not? We're The Disasters, ain't we?'

'Yeah, but we're not The Holocaust.'

'Ain't we?'

'No, Basil, we aren't. What we are though, is number three in the Israeli charts. I think we ought to bear that in mind.'

'Look mate, do the papers wanna know whose shirts *you* wear?'

Distressingly, it looked like they didn't. According to the reviews on-line, which Basil would read out from the back of the tour bus, he was an 'electrifying performer', with a 'real air of danger', and (this one really got to me) 'the charisma and stage presence of a young Jim Morrison.' Conversely, there was never, as Basil was fond of mentioning, any real discussion of anyone much, with regard to my guitar-playing. Routinely, Bambi got more press than I did. Arguably, even Dave had more of a following.

'Can you name the guitarist of The Doors, mate?'

'Of course I can . . . I'm sure I can . . .'

'You're on Mastermind, mate, and the clock's running down . . . the sweat's pouring off your brow . . .'

'Was it Ray something-or-other?'

'Could be. Who knows?'

'The guitarist of The Doors,' Bambi said, sleepily, 'was Robbie Krieger, I think.'

'But are you sure about that, love?'

'No. Dude, honestly, I don't care ... where's the morphine?'

'It's here,' I said.

'Great. Wake me in Berlin, guys.'

'Dave,' I said, flustered by now, 'what do you think about this?'

'Dave ain't listening.'

'I get that. Actually, where is Dave?'

'Fuck knows, mate.'

'Basil can you drop that accent? This is hard enough as it is.'

'What, managing us?'

'It kind of is . . .'

'But who put you in charge?'

'Look, can we talk about this once the acid's worn off?'

This sort of thing used to happen a lot. The tour bus, while not much longer than the average Winnebago, seemed to stretch on indefinitely. Dave could have been anywhere, chopping out lines in the facilities, say, or opening a cheeky breakfast lager, or finishing a level on GTA.

'Seriously Basil, where is Dave? We didn't leave him in France, did we?'

After some discussion, and a couple of phone calls, it turned out we had, in fact, left Dave in France. Speaking from Strasbourg, Dave sounded okay, perhaps even relieved by his plight, if slightly less so when I assured him he was still in the band. On the face of it, it was beholden on us to go back and get him, but –

'You guys are totally delayed already,' said Jens, our driver and roadie, Dutch, tolerant and already tested beyond reasonable limits. 'I am thinking you do not wanna cross the border again, guys? That you should maybe get some new man to play the drums for you?'

'Oh yeah?' said Basil.

'Yes. I have heard your music. I am thinking that, possibly, a child of five could play it?'

I began to say something about our garage rock influences, but perhaps Basil said it best when he observed;

'Yeah, any fucker could do it.'

'And I could be that fucker, my friends.'

'You reckon?'

'I believe so, yes.'

'Okay then mate, you're in.'

'No disrespect, Jens,' I said, 'but are we sure about this?'

'I ain't ditching the morphine.' said Basil.

'Heard that,' said Bambi.

'Well no. Nobody wants to ditch the morphine, but we can't just abandon Dave, can we?'

'Oh just E-mail him or something. Send him a ticket back home on the Eurostar. Ain't we got a manager who can deal with all that?'

'Yeah, yeah . . .'

'In the meantime, mate, I'll handle the ideas. And the poetry.'

If you tour the world on a lot of drugs, a certain amount of backstage drama is inevitable. But while it looked like Dave was going to be fine, the Jewish question had yet to be resolved by the time we reached Tel Aviv, to play our debut gig at an outdoor festival. I suppose I should known something was up, when Basil insisted we go on before him, because he had a surprise up his sleeve. The sleeve, that was, of the vintage SS jacket he'd somehow got hold of on his way through Europe. How had he got it into the country? And how were we, as a group, going to get out? By song three, he was into a rendition of the *Fawlty Towers'*

'Germans' walk. By song five, he'd stripped off the tunic (good) to unveil what looked suspiciously like (not so good) a suicide bomb. Satire, irony – these aren't subjects you want to get into with Israeli stage security. Or the police. Or customs. They don't see the funny side. If it hadn't been for our Jewish credentials, plus Basil's line, in the interviews afterwards, about how he'd been emotionally unbalanced by his trip to Dachau (where, to be fair, he'd dropped half a sheet of blotter acid – I can't even begin to imagine what that was like) we might have spent a few months in a Tel Aviv prison. Which, given his burgeoning Jesus complex, Basil, I reflected at the time, would have loved.

The journey round the world continued. Fortunately, we didn't have to go back through Europe, but there was Australia, then Japan, and then ultimately Thailand. The fans were great, if somewhat irritating – 'Baz we love you!' they kept on shouting, when he was too stoned, or, okay, almost too stoned to know what love meant. There's no democracy when it comes to groupies. But the hotels, the police and especially customs were an ongoing source of anxiety. To the extent that, by the end of the tour, we'd all acquired the traditional accoutrements of a traveling rock group, the raging paranoia, the lifetime bans from international hotel chains, and the festering, soul-destroying, inter-band tensions. There was little we didn't know about each other, by the finish. I'd told Bambi I loved her at least three or four times that I could remember, but we always seemed to end up coaxing Basil down from the twenty first floor balcony of the Holiday Inn It's a strange business at times, as if all you're doing's just playing out a script that was done and dusted well before you were born, while waiting around for someone to die in a bizarre gardening accident.

So the long and short of it was that by the time we arrived back in London to record our next album, we didn't have any songs. Was this a problem? Well in theory, it shouldn't have been. We were never exactly been overburdened with those, and a couple of hit singles will usually get you through. It was just that after Tel Aviv, which was all over YouTube, (as internet-savvy, modern-day rockers we should have thought about this, but we hadn't) there'd been a distinct cooling in relations between us and the record company. Our A&R guy had left, which is never good, but the problem went deeper than that. There had been more sweeping changes.

And then there was our new look. In the Rockstar video game (a tour bus fave) you progress, in stages, from being hip young gunslingers to respected stars, before ending up raddled and out of fashion, like Mötley Crüe at the end of Eighties. And we seemed to have managed it in record time. What shambled into head office was more or less unrecognisable from the short-haired indie kids they'd sent out on the road four months earlier, thanks to the piercings, tattoos and tour bus tans we'd acquired in the process. Bambi, for example, had gone from being a pixie-like Mod to an S&M vision in leather and chains. Admittedly, the look worked for her, but what the rest of us now resembled was burned-out rockers from the LA death metal scene, so marketing, if nothing else, was going to be a challenge.

I was taken aside and asked about Basil.

'What's *wrong* with him?' they said.

I explained about his Dachau experience.

'Right. But he must have got some lyrics out of it, yeah? So let's hear the new tracks!'

'About those . . .'

So they gave us a month to get our act together, or that was it.

And it hadn't always been that way. We'd started out as The Nice Jewish Boys, Basil and I, playing weddings, parties, anything in Hampstead, Hendon Central and

Golders Green. Seeing as The Nice Jewish Boys was, in essence, an art terror project (early songs included *The Shiksa Is Pregnant, I Want A Blue Collar Job* and *Palestine Blues*) we hadn't lasted too long on the bar mitzvah circuit, but that was okay. We were, I suppose, and in time-honoured fashion, in open revolt against our own backgrounds, both strictly religious, Orthodox in my case, doubly so in Basil's, where the emphasis on work, study and prayer didn't sit that well with an artistic temperament. Had acid house, punk or even the the Sixties ever really happened in Golders Green, never mind Stamford Hill? Not according to the community they hadn't. We used to see ourselves as Londoners, Basil and I, just part of the mix, not anything to do with 'some sort of backward-looking, sectarian pressure group'. Or 'religious death cult'. This used to go over as well as you'd imagine at the Sabbath dinner table. So, faith schools and the synagogue were the order of the day, topped off, when we were eighteen, with a gap year trip to a religious kibbutz in the Golan Heights.

In a way, this was life-changing. The website had promised an endless summer, four months picking apples and lemons with dusky model types, in the promised land. There was a tacit suggestion we might even find girlfriends. But kibbutz allocation can be a bit of a lottery. Instead of the mooted paradise, we'd wound up in a blasted encampment on the Syrian border, in what, it turned out, was the start of the winter. Up in the mountains at the time of year, you don't need shorts, shades or sun tan lotion. I dare say it rained for a solid month, from the time we arrived. Nor was the commune super-friendly. The view seemed to be that us pampered, diaspora types should learn a few hard lessons about the pioneering spirit that had built the homeland: Four months of labour in the factories, plastics and chicken, ensued. Coupled with a diet of the sort of Zionist indoctrination (about war and self-sacrifice) that made what we'd heard back at the faith school seem like a walk in the park. We'd start our shifts at four in the morning, then spend the next eight hours making wellington boots for the army's chemical warfare division, or dealing with the poultry. Specifically with killing the things, which can put up a bit of a fight. Approaching an angry bird with shaking hands, while the overseer curses you as 'an English pussy' is an interesting experience.

'You come to Israel, you think you'll pick oranges and fuck our women? No! We fuck your women! And we pay you peanuts!'

The irony here being, of course, that there were no girls in our group. Instead, there were eight of us guys, North London Jews to a man, none of us exactly cut out to be sons of the soil. We were, if we survived kibbutz, probably going to go on to be doctors, accountants, psychologists and so forth. Nice flats in Hampstead, or God help us, Clapham. No wonder the desert warriors hated us, even more than we hated ourselves. I was a plump kid with glasses, and Basil, Morty and the rest weren't any better suited to working life in a terror hot zone, armed guards routinely patrolling the compound, with no real relief from the cycle of drudgery expect to repair, after work, to the volunteer's bar (an air raid shelter downwind from the chickens) to drink away our sorrows on subsidised beer. Four months of this, and all us guys were pretty much fogged, and avowed anti-Zionists, never more so than when our entire group was marched off the compound at gun point, after *somebody*, in a moment of drunken exuberance, had driven one of the kibbutz tractors into the swimming pool.

'Mate,' I recall saying, as the headlights sank under the water, 'they're not going to like this'

'Fuck them.' said Basil. 'I can handle them.'

He was still pissing blood a week later he said, thanks to the hiding he took for his part in this incident. These were combat veterans, they weren't fooling around. Nor was his father, the rabbi, all that impressed when Basil staggered off the plane, drunk again, bloodied but unbowed in a 'Jesus Saves' t-shirt.

'You,' yelled the rabbi, across the concourse, 'you fucking bastard, you shit of the earth, how let my son get like this?'

'It wasn't me . . .' I replied, backing away, as Basil was dragged off into the crowd, and then swallowed up by the family Volvo. Oh terrible fate. The next time I saw him, three months later, he said he'd escaped an arranged marriage by the skin of his teeth. 'A wife, a good job in the community and some children . . . soon all his troubles will be behind him,' had been the word, he said. 'Because then he will have have some real problems!' This followed up by what Basil described as 'a chorus of evil laughter.' No one's going to like the sound of that.

Meanwhile, I'd started a degree at the LSE, with a view (not my idea) to becoming an accountant. Clearly, it was time to write a couple of protest songs, and, as far as it was possible, avoid mainstream society.

And so it was that after a couple of years as The Nice Jewish Boys, honing our craft on the London circuit, specifically its toilets, we managed to get ourselves a record deal. Along the way we picked up Bambi, ('You guys are so fucked up! Can I be part of this?') and later on Dave. We were told to drop the religious material, so we did, and to think of a better name. At which point we began to pursue a more commercial direction, if one still hellbent on giving society the sort of telling-off that it seemed, to us, to so richly deserve. Though I'm not sure anyone was more surprised than Basil and I when it started to look as if society might actually be listening.

But that had been then, this was now. The songs, once free-flowing, didn't come so easily any more. Composing an album in under a month was a bit of a facer. I'm not saying Basil had lost his touch, or that the mordant wit behind *The Shiksa Is Pregnant* had left the building exactly, just that at some stage during the tour he'd crossed the line, apparently, between being the kind of guy who writes druggy pop songs, and the kind other people write druggy pop songs about. His reply, when I told him about the record company's ultimatum? 'The suits can fuck themselves, man.'

This is okay, as a response, but also, it isn't. Should the suits fuck themselves? Well, yeah, but some veneer of decorum has to be maintained, or you're on an indie label.

So, how to deal with all this? Well, ring up Ted's friend a lot, obviously – the plan was I'd lock myself away with a guitar and a tape machine, in the hope that I'd come out the other side with ten new songs of timeless genius. Or ten songs, anyway. Something of a leap of faith of artistic process, the Coleridge/De Quincey option (get loaded and hope for the best – many have tried, and many have failed) but amazingly, it worked. When I left the flat a week or so later, looking not great, admittedly, with the demos for *Dad, I'm Sorry* on tape upstairs, apologetic was the last thing I felt. Who'd have thought it? Not me. Was I ... a real writer? Were we going to be like the Velvets? Why not? Everything was going to be terrific – the riches of the world would soon fall at our feet. *We Deserve It* in particular, the obvious choice for a single, was, though I say so myself, not too shabby. It was like the Bee Gees on really harsh drugs. Perfect for the dissatisfied Twitter generation.

But these were dangerous thoughts.

Because Basil wouldn't, as a matter of principle, sing anyone else's lyrics. From the very beginning, he'd refused to do covers, partly, it's true, because he was often too wrecked to remember the words, but mainly because he was sure, not unreasonably (it's not a bad attitude to have) that he was a better writer, a better poet, than Morrissey, or Lou Reed. And there was no point trying to convince him otherwise. When his *raison d'etre*, by this stage, seemed to be causing mayhem at various night spots in central London, and, when he found the time, our record company. Given the tensions in the group, if I'd even suggested I'd written the album, that would have been it for us guys, I feared. And I didn't want to have to get a job. Can you party like a madman in an HR position in Acton, say? Probably, yes. But only for a limited time. So, if I've sounded blasé so far, now I was worried. Dave could have pulled pints, Bambi (not her real name) would have landed softly, as all foxy girls do. But I couldn't see Basil on the tube every morning, dreaming of a better life, when he'd already missed his shot at the title. And I wouldn't have liked that much, either. What I'm saying is that what I did to fix this, even though it sounds reprehensible, was for Basil's own good.

I figured that if I couldn't remember writing *Dad, I'm Sorry*, then Basil wouldn't be able to remember not writing it, either.

So what I did, though it was agony-ish, was introduce Basil to the delights of the Ted Mann connection, over the course of ten days. We'd go to the pub for the afternoon, then head back to the studio (my flat, basically) and set to work on the album. I'd get the drugs out, wait for Basil to lose consciousness, then copy out my lyrics in Basil's notebook, in his trademark scrawl. What was I doing to my friend? Saving him from himself? In spite of what happened later, I'm going with that.

And I'm going to draw a discreet veil over the recording process. Ted's connection was often there. Cab rides at eight in the morning? It's what a manager does, I felt.

Eventually, there was an emergency meeting at EMI HQ. Basil was indisposed, so Bambi and I went to discuss the situation. Bambi was basically along for the ride, what the record company was up to wasn't something I liked to bother her with, but I figured we might get less of a bollocking if she showed up anyway, as foxy as ever. Really the last word in heroin chic.

'Look, guys,' said Josh, the new person, full beard, shaved head, heavy framed glasses, Paul Smith shirt and designer trainers, no real interest in whether we lived or died. Fine. He was Jewish, though. I hadn't bargained for that. 'This garage rock nonsense is over, yes? Period. We are not putting an album of that out.'

'Who's *we,* man?'

'*We* are the people who pay your fucking wages.'

'Wages . . . I'm pretty sure that's not how this works.'

'Have you read your contract?'

'Well, no, but . . .'

'*Secondly*, there's your behaviour in the studio. It is not acceptable. I mean okay, we've all been there, I had some wild, crazy times back in the Nineties, believe you me.'

'Really?' said Bambi, peaking on her brunch speedball – God, how I envied her.

'Yes, *really*. This is not the Nineties. This fucking . . . depravity. Can you explain it? One of the studio cleaners was in tears the other day'

'Well, we need a couple of joints to be creative?' I ventured.

'We're not talking about a couple of joints though, are we? I'd assumed the rumours were just industry gossip, or you people attempting to hype yourselves in the music press. But they weren't, were they?'

'I suppose not, no.'

'Your singer, in particular . . . and where is he anyway?'

'He's at home in bed, I think.'

'Is he now? I scheduled this meeting for late afternoon so that wouldn't be an issue.'

'He has the flu.'

'Describe his symptoms, then. No wait, let me guess, cold sweat, cramps, the shakes?'

'I'm no doctor, . . .'

'Right. So what are you?'

'I . . . *we* are artists.' I said, unable to look the guy in the eye.

'So here's what's going to happen. I've heard the tapes, and I don't like them'

'You have no soul, dude,' Bambi said.

'I have *the soul* of someone who is trying to save you from yourselves! Can you not see that? How am I supposed to sell this nonsense?'

'Well, what if one of us died?' I said.

'Have got anyone in mind?'

'I suppose I could kill myself . . .'

'I'm not gonna lie to you – that might improve sales . . . are you going to do that?'

'I might kill someone, Josh.'

'Right. So I think there's just about enough that if we get someone professional in remix the whole dog's dinner, it may be salvageable.'

'It's going to be difficult if anyone else gets involved.'

'Why is it going to be *difficult?* Look, there's no way we're going to let you produce yourselves. Put that out of your mind.'

'Okay, but Basil isn't going to like it.'

'Well, he should have graced us with his presence this afternoon shouldn't he? I'm assuming he knew about this meeting?'

'Um, yeah . . .'

'The money's in touring now,' Josh went on. 'We want you to play festivals, and generate a positive atmosphere. This is what the young people want. Why can't you and that other idiot display a modicum of professionalism?'

'Like One direction, you mean?'

'Yes, like One Direction. They're a) popular, and, b) crucially, they do what they're fucking well told!'

'Who,' said Bambi, 'are No Erection, dude?'

'You see that attitude,' barked Josh. 'That's the fucking problem, right there.'

'Get her . . .' said Bambi.

So that was more or less it, as far as the record company was concerned. They'd put the album out, Josh said, but we'd have to look elsewhere for the marketing spend.

'We may have paid for the music,' Josh fumed, 'and I describe *music* in only the loosest terms, but I'm damned if we're going to market it.'

No way back from that really, but we did need an advertising budget. To recap; we'd been told by our record company where to get off, most of the band were incapacitated, and I was managing, or not managing, everything. We were in a desperate position, so, who was I going to call? The precise opposite of *Ghostbusters*, basically.

'Ted,' I said, ringing him, shivering, from the bathroom floor, 'we need help'

'With what, mate?'

'I, uh, haven't caught you in an inopportune moment, have I? Sorry if I have . . .'

'No,' he said, if audibly zipping his strides up. 'But you ain't been over-phoning the Connection, have you? Because I did say . . .'

'Ted, I have, but our problems run deeper than that.'

'What sort of problems?'

I explained, briefly.

'Fucking hell, boy. Impressive work. It took us four albums to get there.'

'Yeah well, it's all downloads now. Everything happens sooner than it used to.'

'Gotcha. All right. Leave it with me, son, and I'll make some calls. For the usual fee, obviously.'

'Ted, if you can sort this out I'll be indebted'

'Yeah. You will.'

A few tense days later, Ted rang back.

'Son, there's a drinks company interested. They like the single, they reckon they can use it an advert, so they'll pay for a video as sweetener. But you've gotta make sure your singer . . . that animal?'

'That animal.'

'Yeah. He has to drink the product, in the footage.'

'Right . . .' I said, knowing it would be, but what else could I do? 'That shouldn't be a problem, Ted.'

Which is why I'd been trying to keep Emma and Ian away from Basil. And why I'd been attempting to keep this thin web of subterfuge under wraps. To no avail really, but I tried.

'So Baz,' said Emma, pushing her hair back, 'who's this woman who broke your heart?'

'What woman?'

'And what heart?' I said.

'Fuck off, man.'

'The one in your songs,' said Emma, focused on the star. 'Those beautiful songs.' He could have been going on about Bob The Builder, and she'd still have been enraptured. 'This lady . . . did she blow you out, Baz?'

'I . . . um . . .'

'You refer to her quite a lot in your lyrics.'

'Er, yeah . . .'

'I broke up with my boyfriend recently . . .'

(Of course, of course, I thought).

'And your words really helped me through it, you know?'

'Did they? What ones in particular? Babe?'

'The one about "the silver line across a moonlit sky, paradise will have to wait" . . . I'm maybe misquoting,' Emma . . . simpered, that's the only way I can describe it. And that actually wasn't the line at all, as far as I could remember. What song was she referring to? *I* had no idea, so it was a bit irritating when Basil said, 'Yeah, I think I really captured something there . . . but I just write this stuff and then sing it, you get me? I don't look back.'

'We'll be touring the album though,' I said.

'Oh yeah?' said Emma, suddenly flint-eyed again. 'How

d'you think you're going to accomplish that?'

'With ... medication?' I ... is there a word that describes the precise moment when you cough and cringe at the same time? If not, there should be. That's what I did. You could put it down to paranoia, or guilt, though I was way past the latter, but however unwarranted the feeling was, I felt dangerously close to being unveiled.

'Baz,' said Emma, 'I don't mean to talk out of turn, but I think you could be carrying a bit of dead weight here.'

'Yeah.' said Basil.

'I agree.' I said.

'Mate, she's talking about you.'

'What?'

'She is,' said Emma.

'I refuse to accept that . . .'

'Look at the state of you. Your arm's like a fucking pin cushion, mate.'

'No, it isn't ... okay, it is a bit ... but I wrote all the songs . . .'

'Of course you did, mate. Of course you did.'

The problem was, the more I said that I had in fact written the songs (which I had) the less likely anyone was to believe it. But what are you supposed to do? 'Actually, Basil's the main guy, the king of The Disasters!' wasn't a statement I was prepared to make.

Emma looked at me like I was a heavy, leather 'bear' at a primary school parents teachers evening. All of a sudden, there was a sense of things spiralling out of control. Did Basil *know*? About the Connection, and so on? And if so, was he prepared to steal my work? Silly question, really.

'Right,' Basil shouted, 'let's do this thing!'

'Finally,' said Seb. 'Okay, everyone in position? Take one.'

'Seb, I dunno how many takes of this are going to be germane?'

'Fuck off. Just play your guitar, you cunt,' said Basil.

'Nobody cares what you think.'

Everything happened very quickly after that. It was a short tune – the chorus, like all the best songs do, went 'I wanna die x5' but I wasn't expecting Basil to take it literally. However, perhaps because he'd overheard some of what I'd might have said to some of the people on the shoot, about whether or not he was anything other than 'a piss artist', he took a bottle of what he'd previously described as 'gay vodka', poured it over my guitar, and then (points for style here) waited until the makeshift Jews strapped him to the cross, before he lit up a cigar. Which he then, after a couple of drags, flicked over to the pool of Russia's greatest (and only meaningful, really) export, which had somehow gathered itself under my feet.

In fairness to the drinks company, there was no fooling around with this stuff. It was a new brand they were hoping to market to South East Asia, or the Middle East. As Basil was crucified, and my Les Paul copy literally on fire, I had a brief vision – was this going to be our greatest moment? 'Judas!' Basil was yelling, all this live on tape, as the on-set emergency services we hadn't hired didn't rush to the stage.

No one involved was injured too badly (a few hours in A&E was as rough as it got, and we were no strangers) but I recall thinking, chased down the road by the blazing rabbis, just before the whole place went up, that it was a good thing we'd finished recording the album.

THE WORST REVIEW OF MY CAREER SO FAR

It was after the tabloids published the location of my unit in Afghanistan (my military unit, that is, not the marital one, although clearly, I was attached to that, too) that I decided I'd better leave the army. It had been good fun, I'd enjoyed mucking in with the regiment, being one of the boys and all that, but being decapitated live on Al-Jazeera seemed too high a price for the guys to have to pay for hanging with the H-Meister. I mean, I know some great clubs, and I always get my round in, but nobody's *that* good a bloke. Plus, we're a bit sensitive about the whole beheading thing, us royals.

So, what to do next? Well, falling out of Boujis every night had a certain appeal, but I'd boffed, or at least tried to boff most of the fillies in there already, and besides, a chap needs an occupation. Charity was out, because after Mum had been taken out the game in Paris that time, I'd had a few issues with the British public. All right, the bloke was mullered, but we've all been there, and would he, I ask you, have been driving at ninety miles an hour if the paps hadn't been after him? Generally, you at least try to stay under the radar, if you've tied a few on.

Anyway, I digress. The point was that I could never

have been the People's Prince. Shit on The People, is largely what I thought, and if that sounds unreasonable, seeing as they're likely to be picking up my bar tab for the rest of my life, well, somebody buys the tabloids. So how would you feel about the great British public, if they'd effectively put the kibosh on your old dear? And if, at the age of eleven, you'd been pretty much forced, by some bloke who'd been to Fettes, yet, to schlep halfway across London behind her coffin, in front of the same TV audience that had basically put her in there? I'm guessing 'pissed off' wouldn't entirely cover it. So to then be denied the outlet for black thoughts and violent urges that a career in the military seems to afford . . . just seemed a bit much. I could have shot pheasants, I suppose. Well, I did actually, quite a lot. But I didn't want to shoot pheasants. Pheasants weren't what I wanted to shoot, at all.

So a job in Charity was a non-starter. And I couldn't have carried on like Dad, as an organic, environmental spokes-bloke, because I'd have never heard the end of it down at the club. Plus, was he really my father? I'd read the tabloid speculation in my early teens. You can probably imagine what that was like. It's always struck me as odd that the same sort of press types who routinely big up the Sex Pistols had a problem, at the time, with the H-Meister's SS uniform. As far as I could see, we'd been coming from the same place, me and the Pistols. Okay, I'd had a few drinks, and I didn't really think about it, but, honestly, did either Johnny, or Sid? They said some terrible things about the QE2, after all, having never even met her. Having never met her over tea, for example, just after a hash bust. I shudder to think what *God Save The Queen* might have sounded like if they had. She can dish out a hell of a bollocking, can Her Majesty.

Anyway, I don't want to go on. Chin up, bluff Prince Hal, all that. The point was that after Afghanistan, it looked like the press weren't going to be happy until they knew where I was, all the time. And I'd always had a flair for drama. I knew what it was like to be on telly in a desperate hour, after all, plus I liked dressing up, so, career-wise, it looked as if the theatre beckoned. That way, whoever it is that reads *The Sun* would have as much of the H-Meister as they could possibly handle, and the papers in general would know where to find me, the Hull Truck or wherever, six nights a week. Just because of the weirdness factor, I wasn't likely to be short of work, at least not to begin with. And if I did get bad reviews, as seemed equally likely, well, dying on stage had to be better than having my head, my old chap, or something else dear to me lopped off, with prejudice, on the North West frontier. Or being car-crashed to death in a tunnel in Paris. So that was the plan.

A few years of training later then (I won't list the places that turned me down. Suffice it to say that getting into drama school's a bit more taxing than making the grade for Eton or Sandhurst) and I was on stage in Arthur Miller's *A View From The Bridge*, playing Rodolfo. If you're unfamiliar, it's a play about Eddie Carbone, a tough-talking Italian-American docker, who's fatally conflicted about his incestuous desire for his niece, Catherine, who my character shags. Catherine, in this production, was played by quite a fine filly, I don't mind saying. Which was the other reason I'd got into acting. As I said earlier, I'd had a well-refreshed go at most of the totty in Boujis by then, six whole seasons of Arabellas. Not always successfully, it's true, but any self-respecting swordsman, royal or otherwise, has to scatter his seed a bit further than that.

So, first night, a packed house, heavy security, even heavier press, anticipation thick in the air, and Catherine and I were about to consummate our forbidden love. When there was a gunshot from the wings.

'Christ, guys,' I remember thinking, 'this isn't the bloody *Sopranos* . . .'

Lights out at this point, and the next thing I knew, I came to my senses bound and gagged, not in a good way, in what looked like a student flat in Acton, or somewhere.

'Bloody hell,' I thought, 'I haven't been kidnapped by al-Qaeda, have I?'

But of course, I had.

God knows how they got me out of there. I mean, nice job guys, in a way, what with all the security. Tear gas, I think, was involved, plus a motorbike ride with an unconscious H-Meister strapped to the back, but I don't know. When I did see the papers, much later on, I was really just looking for reviews of my Rodolfo. Which, necessarily perhaps, were a bit inconclusive.

In the meantime anyway, there was the question of not so much whether, as when the guys were going to kill me. The guys being Abdul, who was a dentist, Karim, who was a law student, and some other bloke who looked a bit like a guard from the Bluewater shopping centre, though we never really bonded. He just used to hit me in the face, when the others weren't looking.

I'll spare you the details of my early incarceration – I had a bag on my head for a lot of the time but basically, I didn't know what to make of these guys. They could have offed me on stage at the Royal Court, but hadn't, so what were they waiting for? The opportune moment to saw the H-Meister's head off, live on the internet? Or were they perhaps having second thoughts? Well, I was no psychologist.

Still, after the bag came off, around day two, and the ongoing diet of prayer and daytime telly began, I think, to get on everyone's nerves (for a while back there, I really did feel like a resting actor) we got onto the subject of religion.

'But don't you think, guys,' I said, once the issue seemed safe to bring up, 'that this is going to end really badly?'

'The Western world will end badly,' replied Abdul,

waving his gun at the bomb in the corner, which, in spite of my military training, I had thus far failed to notice, 'but Allah will prevail.'

'Right,' I said.

'The pure-hearted warrior of Islam,' said Karim, 'will go directly to paradise.'

'Yeah, I've read the Koran. I had to do it for General Studies A level. You get totty on tap and a river of wine for the rest of eternity if you die in action, right? But guys, that sounds like a night out in Boujis. I mean, I do it all the time, and it gets a bit much after a couple of *years* . . .'

I took a hard punch, actually a series of punches for that, but, for whatever reason, it seemed to register. At least, they did stop hitting me, after a while.

'That is the situation in paradise, right?' I coughed.

'You misunderstand the writings of the prophet,' said Abdul.

'Yah, I did get an F. But since you're going to heaven anyway, if . . . sorry, *when* you set the bomb off, what say I make a phone call? I could give you some pointers on what to expect?'

'What?' said Karim.

'But who would you call?' said Abdul.

'A friend of mine . . . look, if I sound a bit off, you can always just shoot me.'

'Yes. But why would you do this thing?'

'Well,' I said, as the Bluewater bloke loomed over me again, cracking his knuckles, 'you don't seem like *bad* guys . . . I just worry the prophet might have seen you coming.'

When, later on, I regained consciousness, I rang my pal Rafe, on Abdul's mobile.

'Rafe, hi . . . yeah, I'm in a situation . . . in Acton, I think . . . yeah, I know, I know . . . anyway, usual finder's fee. What I need is an ounce of the Bonnie Prince . . . actually, better that two, a bag of pills, a crate of Bolly, and Debbi, Candy and Bambi from Babes of Mayfair . . . well, yes Rafe, it *is* fairly urgent . . . good man.'

'My friend,' I explained, 'doesn't really follow the news.'

'That is good,' said Abdul, with an ominous click of his revolver.

I don't mind saying I nearly wet myself a few times, in the hours that followed. I had to get the guys to hide their weapons, and then to produce them, so to speak, all the while hoping Rafe and the ladies wouldn't blow the whole scene. As it turned out, I shouldn't have worried. Debbi, Candi and Bambi were quite used to blowing bonkers Arab blokes (Did I really just say that? I'm afraid I did) but it was a bit nerve-wracking, all the same. So it was with a sense of . . . real victory, then, that I sat there next morning, in the West London dawn, my erstwhile captors asleep in the arms of the most fanciable and expensive escorts in town, no doubt dreaming of white, crystal mountains, and rivers of finest, vintage champagne. They must have felt like they were in paradise, innocents, in their way. So I almost didn't have the heart to phone up Special Branch, and have the guys tortured half to death. Being outwitted by a member of the British royal family can't be easy, after all.

On the other hand though, they had started shooting during my Rodolfo. You expect the odd bad crit, but being tear-gassed, hit round the head and then kidnapped was exactly the kind of thing I'd got into acting to try and avoid. So I made the call.

Ten minutes later though, as the West London cops came steaming round the corner, and on up the stairs, it suddenly struck me that coke, pills and vice girls weren't especially interests al-Qaeda members were known to pursue. And yet the place was littered.

My strides, in a real sense, seemed around my ankles.

As a prince about town, I'd been in scrapes before. If you've followed my career to any extent, then what you'll have read is the tip of a bit of a serious, South Pole monster, but what were the chances of this being hushed up? Between the guys, the Old Bill and Debbi, Candy and Bambi, plus the whopping wad, that is, the wad from Wapping, that was bound to be on the table after what must have felt like a hunt for a national treasure, all past mistakes for the meantime forgotten, if not forgiven, they didn't look good.

So how the hell was the H-Meister going to explain this one away? My worst reviews seemed ahead of me, suddenly.

But inspiration hits in a desperate hour, so, as the door flew in, I said;

'Guys, chill. There's a bomb in the corner.'

'What?'

'It's okay,' I went on, 'I'm pretty sure I've defused it.'

In the stramash that followed, it was surprisingly (and in some ways disturbingly) easy for the H-Meister to sashay down the stairs, past the armed blokes in Kevlar, and head off up the road for a full English breakfast. In the debriefing later, the psychology beak seemed to find this aspect of the whole affair especially troubling but, as I kept on trying to explain, it was fairly straight-forward. I'd had a heavy couple of days, and eggs, B and a few large gins really are the best medicine.

The subsequent report was on the negative side. Ten pages of the thing, and from what I could gather, it was almost as if I was the villain. There was this and there was that about the H-Meister's 'inability to function in social situations, unless he feels in command'. Plus his, my, 'classic, borderline tendencies.'

'Borderline what?' I wondered, but I've never been out with a filly in specs (who knows how these people think?) so, skipping to the end, the long and the short of it seemed to be that the prof thought I 'should be excused from public appearances for the foreseeable future.' Which was fine by me. Zero duties with the pay cheque intact sounded just the ticket. Already, as the report hit the bin, I was picturing an unfettered life in the Scottish Highlands. The H-Meister running wild and free, armed to the teeth in the family tartan. All this just a dream now, sadly.

Because, as Mum, I think, eventually found out, the press can do a U-turn at any moment. And so it was that after the shot of the H-Meister, being papped in a caff while tucking into beans, sausage, black pudding, the works, apparently not fazed, at all by his ordeal at the hands of al-Qaeda (I've given up trying to spell that correctly) the red-tops decided to go with a take on the story I hadn't expected. There were a lot of features about the Dunkirk spirit, and my stiff upper lip. These, then, were the reviews I hadn't been hoping for. I seem to have become what I set out not to be – the People's Prince. The Jack of Britain's hearts. With all that this dubious honour implies. So my schedule's really packed now, with public appearances, sadly not on the stage, and there are armed guards following me everywhere I go, to the point where it's nigh on impossible to meet any totty, at least not in a meaningful way. On bad days, and there are many, (I've just got back from a tour of hospitals, in England's North East) I can't but reflect on how much better off I'd have been if I'd just embraced my destiny and got plastered in Boujis every night.

Bugger, in short then, about sums up my feelings.

LAVENDER BUNNY AND THE NINTH CIRCLE

It was the night before Christmas, and I was drinking alone, in front of the television. On the menu for the evening was a selection of Costcutter's finest, a big bag of crystal meth (it hasn't really caught on here yet, but I liked to think I was ahead of the curve on something) and Nigella Lawson's *Festive Feasts*.

This isn't quite as desperate as it sounds. I had thought, earlier, about maybe going for a beer, in one of the fash media bars up the road in Shoreditch. But for one thing, the weather outside truly was frightful, so much so that Ladbrokes had stopped taking bets on a white Christmas days earlier, in the face of of conditions that had apparently sent the South East's transport network, never the most robust of systems, screaming, finally, over the edge. And for another, if I had gone out there, there was always the chance that I might have been recognised. Or, maybe more to the point, not recognised.

So the telly it was. The telly, and a toast to absent friends.

It had been quite a while since I'd last seen Lavender Bunny. When, at the end of our week on *Celebrity Come Dine*

With Me, he'd left for Stringfellows on the arm of Jodie Marsh. Or, to be accurate, in her Luis Vuitton tote bag. She'd been supposed to bring him back the next morning, but hadn't, and in a way, I'd figured, as the days turned into weeks, and then months, and Jodie still wasn't returning my phone calls, perhaps LB was more contented now? And if he was happy to be once again partying with the lovelies du jour, the crème de la crème from *Nuts*, *Zoo* and *Loaded*, like he had been after our *Big Brother* victory, then who was I to stand in his way?

On the other hand, though, where had this left me? Well, 'buggered' I think, pretty much covers it. After LB's departure, I'd started another novel, the sequel, that was, to *Beer, Football And Shagging*. But without him around to act as my muse, to in some way facilitate the creative process, the old magic, to the extent that it had ever been there, so not much really, according to Will Self, Lord Prescott and the rest of our critics, appeared to have deserted me. Whole nights would go by in front of the computer, when all I'd end up with was a few hundred words about the government, more successful novelists, or friends from college who probably had made better life choices. However much booze I threw at the problem, I couldn't seem to come up with anything good.

What made this doubly difficult to bear was the, to my mind anyway, not uncoincidental flowering of La Marsh's literary career. She'd been talking about writing a book for ages, on Twitter and Facebook (where I'd taken to following her) but without much success. Until, it seemed, that she'd taken possession of Lavender Bunny. Since then, she'd published *The Ugly Duckling: A Memoir*, and was now wrestling with Jordan at the top of the Christmas best-seller lists. As opposed to in the mud, which is where, if you think about it ... well, I refrain from making the obvious point.

So, adding all that up, the collapse of my star, the ascent

of Jodie's and LB's desertion (though I wasn't inclined to think of it as a betrayal. As a small bunny, he couldn't have been expected to master an iPhone) can I be be blamed for getting stuck into the old pharmaceuticals? I must have thought not.

So I'd been drifting a little, only half paying attention, Absorbed by the majesty of the tree in the corner, some tinsel affair I'd picked up at Poundstretcher. But everything swam into sharper focus when, on the screen, Nigella decamped to rural Essex, to give a vision in tattoos, a deep tan and shining red leather a few tips on alternatives to the festive bird.

'So,' said Nigella, as usual displaying an epic rack, of lamb, 'you've got to rub in the oil . . . really get your hands sticky . . . God, I'm getting quite hot already . . .'

'You do realise I'm a vegetarian, Nigella?'

'Yes. I just like doing that . . . anyway, on with the nut roast. So Jodie, it's been a great year for you, right?'

'Nigella, it has,' said La Marsh. 'I have to pinch myself sometimes, y'know?'

'I bet . . . so what does winning the Orange prize mean to you?'

Winning the . . . *what?* I thought. What fresh hell was this?

'Well, I hope it means I'll finally be taken seriously.' Jodie continued. 'Watch out boys! It's the Booker next!'

And in the corner of the screen, on the desk, by the laptop, did I catch sight of a set of pert, bunny ears? A pair of button-black eyes? I think I probably did.

So I finished my drink, I finished the drugs, and then I . . . walked on down the hall, via the kitchen, to the room at the end. Where I ran a hot bath, with a big splash of Radox, ('let your cares melt away') then got into the thing with the toaster, basically.

Goodbye, cruel world . . . let this torment end . . .

The problem is that it doesn't really work like that.

Perhaps to some, the Christian after-life comes as no surprise.

But I can't think who. If the New Testament's to be believed (and on balance, I'd say it's a mistake to ignore it) even Jesus, at the end, had a couple of doubts. Perhaps even Tony Blair occasionally wonders, and maybe, on bad nights, even actively hopes that at the close of play there will be no white light, and no black tunnel, and no bearded figure waiting at the end, with a staff, a ledger and a list of questions. But it's a mistake if he does. Because that's what I was confronted by, Saint Peter, the fisher of men, looking, in this aspect, like a cosmic version of Lord Alan Sugar, in what suddenly felt uncomfortably like a boardroom situation.

'Listen,' I said, 'I think there might have been some kind of mistake.'

'Do you?' said Saint Peter, or Alan. 'Well, for your information, my friend, mistakes are the business of mortal man. I ain't got time for that. And I don't like being questioned. And I don't like bullshitters neither.'

I said something about the pressures of modern society.

'Don't you "secular world" me. You drank a bottle of gin . . .'

'It wasn't the whole bottle . . .'

'Shuddup!'

'I'm just saying . . .'

'No, you ain't. You ain't saying nothing. You drank a bottle of gin, and then a bottle of Merlot, and then you got into the bath with a bloody toaster! What did you think was going to happen?'

'Well, nothing, really.'

'Everybody says that. You have no idea how often I have to listen to that rubbish! But Jean-Paul Sartre, Nietzsche and the rest of your lot . . . they wept like bloody amateurs, right, when they were told where they were going. Which is where you're going, too.'

'But . . .'

'But nothing! You were given an opportunity, and you screwed it up. There was rookie error after rookie error! It was a bloody disaster!'

'But I've got a lot more to offer . . .'

'That about sums you up, don't it, Michael? That's the bloody problem. You thought you could coast through, didn't you? You thought you could sit on the bloody fence! Well I'm sorry, my friend, but that ain't what I'm looking for.'

'Don't say it . . .'

'No, I've heard enough. Michael . . . you're fired!'

After a long, long fall, I landed on waste ground, by the banks of a river, in a thick, grey mist. There's a moment of confusion, but it doesn't last long, Hell being largely as advertised in the paintings, the video games and in Dante's *Inferno*. Flames, towers and the screams of lost souls stretching off endlessly into the distance, as you join the queue for processing, or judgement. It's a bit like being stuck in bank holiday traffic, the people nearby wailing, mumbling incoherently, or shouting into their mobiles as the gates get closer, 'Abandon All Hope, Ye Who Enter', looming up by the dock in sickly reds, bold yellows, as if hovering over a McDonalds drive-through, on an infernal version of the M25.

Still, standing in line on the shore of the river, the river, that was, that looked less like the Styx of classic antiquity than it did an ink-black version of the Thames these days (the landmarks, if mainly on fire, were quite similar, there was Big Ben, the Commons, the Tate Modern and so on) I couldn't help but reflect on how well Hell's transport system seemed to be working, compared to London's. The ferryman, wild of hair and eye, may have called to mind an angry Bob Geldof, demanding everyone's 'fucking money', but you couldn't have said that he wasn't efficient.

And it was the same with the next thing, the raging, many-armed leviathan that rose up over the House of Lords. Which, I was informed by a small voice off to my left, was the judge of all sins, in charge of sending each soul to its final punishment.

'He likes to think of himself as the Karmic Accountant.' the voice continued.

'You,' bellowed the Great Beast, in a granite Scots accent, his tie stained and crooked, his suit-clad tentacles multi-tasking heavily, as a stockbroker type, who'd been standing right by me, was picked up, shaken, then slung into the abyss, 'are a cunt. And you,' he went on, spiking another, 'are a *fucking* cunt. And you,' he continued, 'are next!'

'No, he isn't,' said the voice, 'you're to let Mike pass.'

'Am I indeed?' chortled the Satanic Presbyterian. 'I don't believe I got that memo. And who are the bloody hell are you anyway . . . oh, right.'

'Yes. So shall I do the maths for you, Gordon?'

'I can bloody well do the maths for myself!' roared the myopic colossus.

'Mike,' said the voice, as I was led away, quickly, by the cuff of my trousers. 'While he's distracted, we really should go.'

'Okay,' I said. 'But what are you doing here, Lavender Bunny?'

'Well Mike, I'm a *psychopomp*.'

'What's a *psychopomp*, LB?'

'It's a soul guide, Mike. I know this looks bad, but I have connections.'

He said he was there to walk me through it, 'like Virgil in Dante, Mike', but that it might not be easy, because the only way out was via the basement, on floor minus nine, and he couldn't be sure we'd be unopposed.

'You might not not think it to look at me, Mike, but I

have enemies here.'

'Like Gordon?'

'Mike, it's best if you don't think of him like that.'

He said while what we'd just seen may have acted a lot like the former UK prime minister, it was something quite different. He said that if I could see Gordon as he actually was, I might not like it. And that the same thing applied to any other manifestations of the New Labour front bench we encountered on the way – I was to think of them all as 'extremely dangerous'.

In particular, he said, anything resembling Lord Prescott was to be avoided.

'In death as in life, Mike.'

'Yeah. So about all this, LB . . .'

'Well, Mike,' LB began, 'long ago, he said, he'd been thrown out of Heaven because he hadn't been sure about the way things were going. He said that he and his friends didn't want to sing hymns Mike, all the time. It was boring. Well, you must have been to church?'

'Not recently, LB.'

'You see, you really should have done.'

'I'm beginning to get that.'

'It's like giving up smoking, Mike. Everyone says so when it's too late.'

'I suppose.'

'Anyway, Heaven is terrible. It's like an English, country village Sunday that goes on forever, Mike. Church for breakfast, lunch and afternoon tea, and *Songs Of Praise* at the end of it all. Imagine that for the rest of eternity . . . it's crap, really.'

So after a few of them had stopped going to evensong, LB continued, there'd been trouble in paradise. He hadn't been one of the ring-leaders, he said, but when the rest had been thrown out, he'd been thrown out with them, and sentenced, along with the others, to tormenting the damned, keeping the hellfires burning, or walking the earth in search of lost souls.

'Hang on, lost souls?'

'The easily tempted. Mike.'

'Right, but I don't see . . .'

'Well, you were no Hemingway, Mike. You were no James Joyce. You probably weren't even the next Tony Parsons . . .'

'LB, I know we're in Hell, but if you could spare my feelings a bit . . .'

'But you wanted to be a famous, Mike, and you wanted to be a tortured artist. So I thought I'd help you along, a bit. I think I did quite a good job.'

'Yeah . . .'

'Mike, don't be like that. You went on *Big Brother*, and *Celebrity Come Dine With Me*, and you did get your book published. None of that would have happened if it wasn't for me.'

'None of it?'

'No. But Mike, you did get what you wanted.'

'Just not in the way that I wanted it, though.'

'Mike, I don't make the rules. The thing is that Heaven doesn't intervene, but it's not true that prayers are always unanswered. It's just that when they are, it's not usually to do with a sick relative. We don't really handle those sorts of requests. But if you want a career in business, or in telly or something, then you never know, there might be somebody listening.'

'Right.'

'Though I've been doing this for a long time, and it doesn't get any easier . . . can you see the construction work, over there?'

'Yeah,' I said, gazing across at what looked like versions of the Shard, the Eye and the Westfield shopping centre, along with other Promethean developments that were going up along the river, the property companies still apparently trying to out do each other, even in Hell, in terms of spoiling the view. 'There seems to be a lot of it.'

'Well yes, there is.'

Because they were having enough of a problem, he said, with the first wave of Baby Boomers, who'd barely arrived yet. Once the oil men, stockbrokers and so on showed up en masse, he continued, things were going to be difficult.

'If everyone stops believing in God, it's only good for us up to a point. Finding the space is going to be hard, and then there's the customer service.'

He said that while it was all right for Bohemian types like he and I to sit around drinking wine, smoking cigs, and so on, because it wasn't as if we were going to do anything about it, the modern business world's endorsement of existential nihilism was more of a worry.

'It's *arbeit macht frei*, Mike, all over again. And say what you like about National Socialism, at least most of them realised they'd done something wrong. Whereas next lot ... will be demanding upgrades, Mike, upgrades, warm toilet seats and to speak to a lawyer the minute they arrive.'

'But shouldn't that be a good thing, LB? To set them all straight?'

'Mike, there are more lawyers here every day. When people like Donald Trump start turning up, we're going to be swamped with complaints. And who's going to deal with all the paperwork?'

'You have paperwork in Hell?'

'Mike, of course we do.'

'Yeah ... actually, why did I ask that ...'

'We have contracts and everything. How could we not? So I think I'd rather get out of here, all things considered, before the trouble really starts.'

'But how are you going to manage that, LB?'

'We should talk about this later. In the meantime, Mike, we'd better keep going.'

And so, we did. After a while, it became easier not to look. Hell, LB said, conformed to certain expectations. But while the major landmarks remained the same, the city, the river, the department store structure, (menswear, murder, leather goods, treachery) the place had nevertheless been modernised, since Dante's time. The damned, these days, weren't so much sentenced according to their sins, he said, it was more a question of what they'd done for a living.

'But I was only a writer.' I said.

LB said that while that was debatable, I might have got away with a few decades in purgatory.

'Oh come on, LB, the book wasn't that bad . . .'

If, he continued, giving me a hard stare, I'd shown a bit more restraint. Because regardless of the strengths, or otherwise, of *Beer, Football And Shagging*, suicide was still considered a big, fat, mortal no-no.

'Oh.'

'Yes, *oh*. So you're not to look back, or we're in serious trouble. You must stop thinking this is all about you.'

And so down we went, through the vaults of damnation, as if via the stairs of an endless shopping centre, as re-imagined by Norman Foster, Damien Hirst or the Chapman Brothers. Past the branches of Starbucks, Ikea and HSBC. Perhaps it's enough to say that accountancy, law and investment banking aren't necessarily the desirable career choices they might initially seem to be. Also, stay out of sales, if you can possibly help it, and that's especially true of financial services.

One thing that hasn't changed since Dante's day, though, LB went on, is that the depths of Hell are still reserved for the political classes.

By about floor minus seven, then, I had a definite feeling that we were being followed. There seemed to brogues and high heels, thundering footfalls, a cloud of dandruff and Christmas aftershave trailing behind us. So much so that by the time we arrived in the ninth circle, at what really did look like the end of the line, the exit glimmering though the thick, red smoke, I couldn't help, finally, but look over my shoulder. At a sight that was enough to turn anyone into a pillar of salt. Hazel Blears, Jack Straw and Alastair Campbell, Prescott aggressively leading the charge.

'Mike, I did ask you not to do that.'

'But I thought you said you were connected, LB?'

'I am, Mike. I am, but . . .'

'So wassup, Lord Beelzebub?' observed Tony Blair, or *Lucifer actually*, as LB described him, who'd now appeared on the floor straight ahead, towering above us in ball-crushing cords and a burgundy tent shirt, seemingly leading damnation's front bench. 'Nice try.'

'Mike,' LB said, 'you should make a run for it.'

'Yeah. Are you going to be all right though?'

'Don't worry about me, Mike,' LB replied, a small figure framed in the lights by the exit, against the advancing horde of unholy bean counters. 'I'll be okay.'

So I woke up freezing, an unplugged toaster in the water next to me. There was a lump on my skull from where I must have slipped over, getting into the bath. On the TV, *Songs Of Praise* was ringing out for Christmas morning. Strange dream, I thought. Perhaps best to lay off the booze for a while though, all the same. Walking next door to start clearing up, and wondering about starting a couple of charity standing orders, just be on the safe side, I was a bit . . . taken aback to see a familiar face on the living room sofa, looking fairly roughed-up and scorched round the edges.

'That was all a bit much, Mike. Can you pour me a drink?'

'Of course. A large scotch and soda?'

'That would be good, yes.'

'LB,' I said, once I'd done the honours, 'I'm glad you're okay, but seeing you here like this . . . does raise some questions about my sanity.'

'I wouldn't worry about that, Mike. It's hardly the first time is it? What was it the publishers said, when you first submitted *Beer, Football And Shagging?*'

'Let's not get into that.'

'I think it's germane. Mike.'

'I don't think it is.'

Anyway, the long and the short of seemed to be that LB was going to have to stay out of Hell for a while. But that was okay, he said, because he'd be able to help with the writing again.

'There's to be no more fooling about, Mike. I see the new book as a hit this time. A best-seller, like Jodie's.'

'Sure, but, how are you going to pull that off? The last one didn't exactly set the charts on fire.'

'Yes Mike, but that was before.'

'Before what?'

'Mike, you should trust me on this. You're not the first who's been through this process, you know.'

'What process?'

'Well Mike, Philip Larkin was a friend of mine, and so was James Dean. And Mephistopheles in Christopher Marlowe's play was based on me.'

'Really?'

'Well, sort of. Marlowe was prone to exaggeration.'

'Right,' I said, as I got up out of the sofa to refresh our drinks.

'Mike, don't you believe me?'

'I can't help wondering if I'm still in the middle of an overdose, LB.'

'Would it help if you saw me as I really am?'

'Probably not, no,' I said, but it was too late, as he began his transformation. His expansion. From a cute foot high to eight times the size, until there was a weighted, shadowy presence on the living room sofa, as if Francis Bacon, Hieronymus Bosch, or one of those other visionaries of damnation had collaborated on a once-seen, never to be shown again out-take from the Sooty Show. It was not a pretty sight.

So when, to whatever debatable degree this applies, I regained my senses, LB, back to normal, was floating about with a stiff glass of gin.

'Convinced now?'

'That I'm not still on drugs? Many wouldn't be.'

'Mike,' he said, rearing up in the air, 'don't make me do that again.'

'No . . . I mean, yeah . . . yes, I believe you.'

'Good. So you know when I said that I didn't like my job, Mike? That it's not easy being a lord of Hell? Because it's too hot, and the office politics are terrible?'

'Yeah.'

'Well, the thing is, you don't have to do it all the time. There's a bit in our contracts . . .'

'You have contracts . . . of course you do.'

'Well, we do. And can you stop interrupting?'

'Sure.'

'Right. So the arrangement is that if you can save a soul from Hell, like I just did . . .'

'Hang on, *saved*? LB, I wouldn't have gone there in the first place if it hadn't been for you.'

'Mike, that's not true. Of course you would. Perhaps I sped things up a bit, but trust me, you were doomed.'

'Really?'

'Yes. So, as I was saying, Heaven isn't totally unforgiving. There's a redemption clause in the legal stuff. Basically, walk a soul out of there and you, don't have to go back, for the duration.'

'The duration?'

'For the lifespan, Mike.'

'And that's the deal you made with Pop Larkin and Jimmy Dean?'

'Mike, they weren't that different from you, really. They were lonely bedsit drunks, who needed a push. They weren't really going anywhere until they met me. I think I've explained about this.'

'I'm not sure you have, LB.'

'Yes Mike, I *have*.'

'Okay ... so ... you'll be with me from now on? Haunting my dreams?'

'Yes. You should see this as more of a positive thing though, Mike.'

'But then what were you doing at the gates of Hell at the precise point I, err, died, LB? If that's what I did ... shouldn't you have been at Stringfellows? What would have happened if we'd never met? If we hadn't gone into the *Big Brother* house?'

'I can't see the future, Mike. I can only guess. But after *Beer, Football And Shagging* didn't find a publisher, you'd have tried to write another novel. But you'd have started to take your job more seriously, as well, and then met a nice girl, like Jodie, and settled down. You wouldn't have liked that.'

'Well ...'

'No Mike, you wouldn't.'

'LB, would I have ended up drunk and suicidal on Christmas Eve, in the year when Jodie won the Orange Prize?'

'You'd probably still have got drunk, Mike.'

'Yes, all right, but otherwise ...'

'Maybe not.'

'LB, would Jodie have won the Orange Prize at all, if it hadn't been for your intervention?'

'Mike, you're focusing on the wrong things. Some people might say that I've done you a favour. At least you know it's there now. Plus, saving a soul from Hell isn't easy, you know. The others don't like it.'

'What others?'

'Lucifer, Asmodeus, the demon Pazuzu ... well, you've met them. They think I'm a bit of a dilettante, Mike. Who should be getting on with the serious work of torturing the souls, and not always trying to shirk his responsibilities . . . but it takes a certain flair to find solitary types, get them to commit suicide, and still have them trust you enough to follow you out of there. I think the others are jealous.'

'I bet they are.'

'And anyway, was it all bad? I quite enjoyed myself, anyway. Running around with Jodie, having a wild time.'

'I was going to ask about that.'

'Mike, if I hadn't betrayed you with Jodie, you might not have killed yourself. And then where would we be? All my efforts would have been in vain . . . no, don't look at me that way . . . they would have been.'

'LB, I'm beginning to reassess our relationship.'

'But why Mike? You're still alive, aren't you? And we should be okay, for the next however many years. What are you, twenty eight? We have decades ahead of us. And I'll be looking out for you, every step of the way.'

'Like you were for poor old Jimmy Dean?

'He was a sensitive man, Mike.'

'Couldn't deal with it?'

'Not at all. Philip Larkin, though, lived to a ripe old age.'

'But wasn't he on sixty cigs and a bottle of vodka a day, by the end?'

'Nobody's perfect, Mike. Nobody's indestructible. All you can do is give it the old college try.'

'I suppose.'

I poured us out another couple of cocktails, shaken, of necessity, and not stirred. What could I add? We clinked our glasses.

'Merry Christmas, LB.' I said.

'God damn us one and all, Mike!'

INVESTMENT OPPORTUNITIES ON THE ISLE OF MAN

How to explain about Mr Funny?

It's not a particularly easy task.

Was Mr Funny a kind man? Was he a humanitarian man? Perhaps only in the sense that he'd sometimes talked about kidnapping our business rivals, putting them 'in a frikkin' hog oven', then serving them up with 'mash potatoes and apple sauce' the 'goddamn, ingrate, limey faggots'. He used to see himself as a Donald Trump figure. Just a dreamer, really. A 'regular, blue-collar *schlub* from the wrong side of the tracks', who 'hadn't gone to no fancy college', and who wasn't prepared to 'sit around on his goddamn *keister*, waiting for the big shots to throw him a bone.' Certainly, when it came to striking a land deal, no one accused Mr Funny of letting the grass grow under his feet. Though he did make an exception for the golf course, I guess. The greens, he'd say, outlining his vision in one of our meetings, would be fertilised by not just 'the hearts, the guts . . . the frikkin' ground-up skulls of our competitors, but also 'their frikkin' children, Davey, if the mothers don't play ball!'

'Right, but . . .'

'Ah, shut it, Davey. Shut ya fuckin' mouth!'

So I was troubled, I admit, when I took to the stage on that sun-drenched, waterside, afternoon. The hotel, the casino, the Nineteenth Hole, in fact everything to do with the marina development that was, Mr Funny and I hoped, finally going to bring the Isle of Man into the twenty-first century, drugged if necessary, metaphorically speaking, depended on what happened in the next forty minutes. Months of planning had gone into this, and we'd laid on a lunch. So the island's great, it's good and its not-so-good (perhaps especially the latter, if the footage I'd seen was anything to go by) were assembled on the quay. Mr Funny once said that the Isle of Man's political scene was like an evergreen bowling club, if everyone involved was 'a goddamn Nazi', and there was a lot of pastel out there, a lot of leathery skin. There was a parliament of lizards out on the dock, but while palms had been greased and, as Mr Funny put it, 'assholes had been lubed', I was still unsure about my presentation. This is the trouble with having a silent business partner: draw up the agreement as clearly as you like, you still never quite know when he's going to speak up.

So I'd first met Mr Funny in downtown Manhattan, in the late October of 2006. In what I wish I could say was a prescient step, I'd taken voluntary redundancy from Lehman Brothers, having made a couple of trades that even in terms of the market back then, were considered not far off the acts of a terrorist, or, perhaps worse, a Radiohead-listening, anti-capitalist douche. Seeing as Lehman Brothers, famously, weren't that big on acknowledging failure, at least in public, I had been given my golden handshake. But it had been made fairly clear, during my leaving do, that what I should have been given was a golden kick in the ass, and that my days on Wall Street as a senior trader, or in fact as anything senior to a toilet trader, were now over.

So, surfing the net on that fateful Friday, I was looking round, long-term, for new career opportunities. And also, in the short-term, for a Halloween costume for the party that night. I wouldn't usually have been after a full-face mask, because as a single guy dressed up as Spider-Man or Leatherface, even from the neck up, you may as well stock up on a few cans of Special Brew, and order your lonesome cab home before the night even starts. Still, on this occasion, when former work colleagues were sure to be attending, a disguise of some sort seemed a solid investment.

So I'd found this shop, deep in the Village. Later, I was asked where I'd managed to get such a 'butt-ugly' mask. Tellingly perhaps, the place where I bought Mr Funny isn't there any more. But they had quite a selection. Leftover stuff from Goth rock videos, Marilyn Manson, Slipknot, that sort of thing. Gimp masks, torture masks, masks with nails hammered in. Masks with appendages so distended they could have been props in the kind of underground, experimental adult films that are best not thought about. Basically, it was downtown. There were all kinds of horrors. But there was something about Mr Funny, about his twisted, scary clown leer, that seemed to speak to me somehow. He looked blue-collar basically, like a janitor from hell. So, in the spirit of irony, I suppose, given the way my career prospects looked, I got my credit card out.

Anyway, the party was fine. From what I recall (not that much, it's true) Mr Funny was something of a hit. Certainly, nobody asked me to clean up afterwards. But, although this hasn't been covered in any of the books yet, the Lehman Brothers party set was prone to extremes. At the bash there were pills, there was coke, there was angel dust, so much so that I lost track of time a bit, before coming to my senses in the meat-packing district at three in the morning, while attempting to negotiate with what a strange, rasping voice in the back of my mind referred to as 'a frikkin' fine slice o' *tuchas*.'

'Honey,' said the lady, 'I'll make you feel sooo good . . . but it gonna be extra, if you wearin' that thing.'

'What thing?'

'Fool, fuck you! You so outta yo head, you don' even know? Irv? Yo Irv, come over here and fuck this motherfucker up! Fuckin' stupid-ass whiteboy motherfuckin' clown . . .'

'Okay, okay . . .' I said, if feeling a bit muffled or abstracted and unsure about the etiquette – I had no idea what I was agreeing to really, but still, 'A deal's a deal.' I went on. 'I suppose.'

'So, baby . . . ?'

'Erm, your place or mine?'

'Motherfucker, dressed like that, y'all best believe we goin' to *my* office.'

'Yeah, I suppose my place is a bit off-limits.'

'Oh yeah? Where you work, honey?' said the courtesan, perhaps now for the first time registering the Armani, the Rolex. 'Uptown, maybe? Y'know, if ya pour on some more sugar, we could do it on ya desk? Y'all like that, honey? Yeah, I'm feelin' you would . . .'

'Perhaps,' I said, as she checked my credentials, so to speak – do I have to spell this out? 'My pass card is still effective . . .'

'Lemme see . . . ooh, no doubt, baby. No doubt . . . y'all got a key to the executive washroom!'

The next morning, I woke up with a thumper behind the eyes. There was a feeling of latex glued to my anatomy. Ah, wild, crazy nights. Half-asleep, on auto-pilot really, I made my way to the facilities.

But in the mirror, past the overturned furniture, the graffiti on the walls, I was confronted by Mr Funny. He said;

'Davey, ya gone to the frikkin' john in ya pants here.'

'Where is here?' I said, talking, but also not talking to myself, in effect. To the spectral, red-eyed presence in the glass. This is difficult to explain.

'Davey . . .'

'Dave,' I said. 'It's Dave.'

'Fuck you, ya fuckin' mook. Now here's the thing. You nailed a hooker in ya goddamn office, and then you wrote all this crap on the paintwork . . .'

'What crap?'

'Look at it, Davey.'

I looked around. Emblazoned on the walls in magic marker were lines like 'Seinfeld was the Baptist, and Trump the Christ! But Mr Funny is God!'

'I don't remember any of this.' I said.

'Okay, maybe you were nudged a little. But we gotta get outta here now. Where you from?'

'Where am I . . . from?'

Mr Funny reared up in the glass.

'All right, steady on. The Isle of Man.'

'Where the fuck is that?'

'Britain, sort of.'

'The land of faggots and warm frikkin' beer? So be it, I guess. Okay, Davey . . .'

'*Dave* . . . Jesus Christ.'

'Don't get ya panties in a frikkin' bunch. You gotta passport, yeah?'

'Mm.'

'Best pack ya bags then, Davey.'

'Why, exactly?'

'Mr Funny's too pretty. You know what happens to guys like me in jail?'

Some facts about the Isle of Man, then. This, from Wikipedia, is the kind of thing I'd put in the brochures.

'The Isle of Man is a low tax economy, with no capital gains tax, wealth tax, stamp duty or inheritance tax, and a top rate of income tax of 20 per cent. A tax cap is in force. The rate of corporation tax is 0% for almost all types of income.' Add some bumph about the scenery, the golf and the excellent restaurants, and you're almost bound to attract a certain clientele. I mean, it sounds great, doesn't it?

And to begin with, it was. From my time at Lehman's, I'd salted away enough of a stake to establish myself in the island's property market. You buy a couple of houses for cash money down, and after that, you keep on flipping them, or using them as security from ever more elaborate and fantastical developments, until you're a player, was the plan. In a small place like that (population 80,000) it's only a matter of time. And the market was going like a fair back then, or perhaps even a circus. We went from flats to a hotel ('La Commedia', we called it, in homage to Mr Funny's Italian roots) to more grandiose schemes, specifically our golf course, in surprisingly short order.

Until, that was, we hit a bit of a glass ceiling. As an outsider, and this is doubly true if you aren't in the Masons, there's an issue of space. However much money you throw at the problem, there's only so much lebensraum to go around. And we were by no means the only developers in town.

And as with all great visionaries, Le Corbusier, Albert Speer, Donald Trump, Mr Funny wanted everything done yesterday. He wasn't content to wait about 'like an asshole', while the wheels within wheels of our planning applications ground their sleepy way on. So as our great lost golf course, planned for an island that was, admittedly, already littered with the things, became increasingly mired in its own legal sand trap, he began to talk about blackmail. About oiling the committee with poison if necessary, 'if the mothers won't take cash!'

'But some of them really are mothers . . .'

'Oh yeah?' he'd seethe from the mirror, 'You tell 'em I'll fuck 'em all anyway.'

Drugs, prostitution and gambling debts were mentioned. In a town like Douglas, the island's capital, discretion's usually the watchword when it comes to vice – it's not supportable otherwise, the neighbours do tend to talk – but Mr Funny wouldn't listen.

'Mr Funny,' I'd say, 'this isn't the most interesting place to grow up. People generally get a flight to the mainland, if they're for looking that kind of action.'

'Yeah?'

'Yeah.'

'Then maybe it's time for a coupla changes.'

So as the marina development became the focus of our efforts (because where could we go now, except into the sea?) I started to suffer from blackouts again. Whole days would go missing. Strange business cards and mysterious wraps smeared with white powders would often be there on the bedside table, as I woke up into the confusion of dawn. It was all uncomfortably like the last days in Manhattan.

But I hadn't been quite sure what he was up to until a few days before the presentation, when I'd gone out for lunch with potential investors. I'd locked Mr Funny in the cellar at home, just to be on the safe side, but had, nevertheless, still come to my senses an indeterminate time later, back at the mansion, in the midst of spiking the punch with Viagra or something, while nubile young things with Estonian looks cavorted in the pool with key island luminaries, and Mr Funny held court, like a lord of misrule from darkest New Jersey. And the closed-circuit cameras whirred away in the background.

At this point, Mr Funny and I repaired to the study, for an emergency meeting. Item one on the agenda was who in the hell was running this company.

'It's not just a business, it's my brain!'

'Fuck you, Dave! You ain't got no balls! Lemme show ya sump'n . . .'

126

And so to item two on the agenda: the somewhat lurid footage Mr Funny had acquired, both there at the mansion, and in the low-end house of ill-repute that he'd apparently, and quite impressively, managed to turn La Commedia into, the bar now littered with vice girls, it seemed, shipped in in from the mainland for special, costume parties.

'How,' I said, a trifle dumbfounded, as the DVD images flipped from room to room, 'have you managed to do all this?'

'Ah come on now Davey, ya gotta take some of the credit.'

'Oh. Oh shit . . .'

So there I was on the dock, a day or two later, preparing to share our vision. In my pocket, there were two DVDs. Disc A, my work, listed the benefits the marina would bring to the island. Disc B, on the other hand, was a quite different kind of poolside production. But as to which was which, or who'd be conducting the post-presentation Q&A session, once the film had been shown, on the forty foot screen looming over the dock, well, who knew, I wondered, as I straightened my tie, and approached the stage.

'Are your lives pure? Are your lives decent?' rang out the voice, almost like a strange man shouting from the pavement, as the long, black car I was sat somehow in the back of pulled away, gently, and over the side. 'You fuckin' assholes, here's how it's gonna be!'

THE NEW DOCTOR

'Yeah, but I think I could get off with her,' I, Matt Mitchell, said, flicking the long, lustrous fringe back off a face that, while maybe not that conventionally boy band handsome, was still soon to be famous all round the world, if not the universe. 'Let's face it, I'm a timelord. I can do what I want.'

'I don't think so.' Georgia, the actress playing my daughter said, eyeing me from across the console as if I was a Cyberman or something. An inhuman monster.

'Yes,' said Russell, the old producer, in his grating Welsh accent. 'For one thing, the Doctor doesn't just *get off* with anyone. And for another, *Mr* Mitchell, in this incarnation you aren't going to *have* a love life. You're going to be more cerebral. More . . . what's the word? Oh yes, Emo.'

'Right. So it was okay for Eccleston and Tennant to have birds falling all over them, but not me?'

'We feel you have different strengths,' said Russell, with a nasty smile.

'But didn't you want to cast Tilda Swinton? What d'you think that would have meant for the Doctor's relationships? The one with Piper, especially? It doesn't sound like teatime viewing to me.'

'*Billie* Piper,' hissed the Welshman, 'left the programme several series ago. Or *didn't you know*?'

'Look mate,' I said. 'I'm a serious actor. You don't think I actually watch this stuff, do you?'

'Okay,' said Russell, his ample chest heaving under the damp, stretched fabric of his Tom Baker t-shirt, while the lights and machinery buzzed away in the background. As the Doctor, I reflected, I was soon to be facing down the horrors of the cosmos on a weekly basis, but there were limits. 'Well, while we're on the subject of your *acting*, I don't think the Method approach is what's required here. It's a family show, yes? You're not in *Raging* bloody *Bull*, you know.'

'From where I'm sitting, that's open to question.'

'Are you saying that I'm *fat*?' raged Russell.

'Well, you said I was ugly.'

'I did *not*.'

'Yeah mate, you did. You said, and I quote, "If that bloody minger is allowed anywhere near my beautiful TV show, I shall thuh-row myself under the wheels of a London omnibus."'

'I did not say . . . all of that . . .'

'I did see the e-mail Russell.'

Look, I know what you're doing here. Don't think I don't. Trying to undermine old Russell, aren't you, you little sod?'

The console hummed to itself for a while. There was steel in the Welshman's eyes. Possibly, I was on thin ice here. But if I was going to make my mark on this part, and hopefully, I was, then it seemed important to establish that as far I was concerned, David Tennant's Doctor was a dead man. To put as much distance as possible between his interpretation of the character and mine. This, admittedly, in spite the age-defying good looks and personal charm he'd brought to the role.

'So,' I went on, taking advantage of the silence, 'seeing

as my daughter was technically fathered by Tennant's incarnation, I think it'd raise some interesting questions if . . .'

'A clone,' broke in Georgia. 'Your daughter is a clone.'

'A what?' I said.

'It means,' she said, 'that you'd effectively be trying to have sex with yourself. Probably not for the first time.'

'Right,' I said, as I helped myself to a can of Stella from the case I'd dragged in earlier on a trolley – I'd introduced it to everyone as K-12. 'Well, I don't have a problem with that.'

'This is not,' snapped the Welshman, 'how I see the new Doctor, at all.'

'How do you see him then, Russell?' I asked, in the certain knowledge that he'd wanted a long list of actors, Tilda Swinton in particular, but really anyone except me, to play the part instead. That he wasn't at all happy with the idea of a no-nonsense, geezer Doctor. That it was only the late-Seventies, David Bowie haircut McTavish insisted on that had swayed him otherwise.

'He should be a sympathetic figure.'

'But mate,' I said, as the latest beer, *K-4* I supposed, slipped through time and space to the floor of the Tardis, where I'd insisted the meeting be held, 'what gives you the idea he won't be?'

'Matt, *lovey*,' said Russell, eyeing the lager pooling on the tiles, 'it's ten o'clock in the morning.'

'Yeah, but if you know your Who lore, you'll know that Tom Baker spent a lot of time in the pub with Francis Bacon.'

'I don't feel as if your work will be in any way comparable.'

'To Francis Bacon's? Oh, probably not. But I like to think he'll be an influence.'

'Shut *up* . . . just shut up!' bellowed the Welshman. 'Look, you're not an artist, you're a fucking little bumboy!'

'Well, I don't think I am . . .'

'Listen, you floppy-haired *tit* . . . this could be a career-defining role for you. Play your cards right, and in twenty years' time, you might even make landlord at the Queen bloody Vic . . .'

'Great.' I muttered.

'So I don't understand why you're being so ungracious. Your behaviour is *not* acceptable.'

'Right. Do *you* want to explain that to the fans though? Because I'm not going to.'

'Oh God,' said the Welshman, placing his head in his hands. 'Still,' he went on, as if remembering the kind of plot twist that routinely saves the Doctor at the last minute, and gazing over, as he did so, at the figure in the corner, who hadn't said much so far. 'Stephen, this is your problem now. I bow out gracefully.'

'Christ,' I said. 'This really is a show about sci-fi isn't it?'

'I will see you, boyo, on the way back down . . .' Russell said, as he stormed out of the Tardis. And then back in. 'Look Stephen, I really feel like you're making a big mistake . . .'

'Mm.' said Steve, who was taking over production at the start of the new series. Like me though, he was a bit concerned about that. When it came right down to it, was Russell, after all those years of awards and acclaim, really going to be able to leave the time machine behind him? Conceivably, as Steve would sometimes say, the 'fat nutter' would be back on set 'in the flash of a Dalek's undercarriage' the minute his new projects ran into trouble.

'He's been doing what he wants for quite a while now.' Steve would continue, with a haunted air. 'I've got a feeling he's going to find it hard to adjust.'

So I wasn't the Doctor for that long, in the end. Has anyone else lasted just a series? Or met with such a lovingly-crafted and agonising demise? Fans of the show may well have wondered why my Doctor spent the first half of his last episode with a sack on his head in a Martian jail, before being 'ray-gunned to death in the sewers beneath', as the script put it, and then rising again in a new, almost Christ-like incarnation. If so, I suppose all I can say is that in any long-running TV series, particularly a smash like the *Doctor Who* revamp, the handover's bound to be difficult. That the old producer, while accepting, on the face of it, that he has to let go of his baby, still wants to make sure the kid's in good hands. That he doesn't want to feel as if it's been packed off to boarding school, or an abusive foster home. But that equally, the new guy in charge has to break with the past, or what's the point? Conflict, in this situation, is basically a given.

So I was feeling a bit rough, but also ready for the challenge, by the time I rolled into the Tardis, for the meeting that morning. I'd been told, by McTavish, that I should go to bed early the evening before, but after *Murderous Maniacs* I was so at odds with the tartan beast that even this, on the face of it fairly reasonable advice, had fallen on deaf ears.

'The point, laddie, is not to traumatise the audience.'

'But isn't that exactly the point?'

'The viewers at home are supposed to be hiding behind the sofa because of the monsters, and not the Doctor.'

'Yeah ... that's really not the plan, mate. I don't think I'll be posing for any calendars.'

'You have to make things bloody difficult, don't you Michael?' McTavish sighed.

So the life of a struggling actor is ... well, it's a struggle. For fairly obvious reasons, I hadn't done much telly since *Murderous Maniacs*, so I wanted to make the most of this, my first proper job in ages. Basically, I had to make a splash.

Because how to follow the handsomest Doctor? At

least without crash-landing the Tardis as badly as someone like Colin Baker had, in the Eighties? I was under no illusions about our relative viewer appeal. In fact when I'd signed the contract, Steve had called me into the office, and shown me Tennant's fan mail, two bulging sacks of it.

'You can forget about those, mate,' he'd said, 'with your look. No, a fresh vision's called for. A radical approach.'

So what, I'd asked, did he have in mind? But I think I already knew.

The initial episodes were a bit tricky. There was a certain amount of to-ing and fro-ing about the new direction. But after I gave the writers my coke dealer's number, there was less of a problem than you'd think with the Doctor being enough of a morally ambiguous figure to, say, shave his head and start getting into fist fights, It wasn't exactly teatime viewing, but it did stand to reason that if the Doctor changed his look and persona with each incarnation, to the extent of being credibly re-imagined as a black or female character, as Russell had planned, then sooner or later he could be a bit of a villain, too.

Fave scene out of all of them is towards the end of the, perhaps ill-advised, *Return Of The Cybermen* episode when, as I step away from the smouldering mine shaft, my new assistant Debbi (Georgia, by this point, had left the series) brushes the black dust out of her long, blonde highlights, her crop top and mini skirt, and says;

'Doctor, I love you. But sometimes you can't solve a problem with words, mate! Sometimes you gotta get stuck in!.'

'I know, Debs.' I say, reloading the shot gun, 'I know. All right then, you dirty little sods!' I yell at the robots. 'Let's be 'aving you!'

I suppose everybody knows what happened later.

I'm still not sure who was leaking the stories (Georgia, perhaps, or had Russell slipped some cash to a moody

Cyberman, to tell tales out of school?) but the upshot was that it all came out. The disastrous focus groups, the bust-ups on set, 'Doctor Booze!' on the front page of *The Sun*, after I mistook Davros for a futurist lavatory, that time. My concept for the role was a young Grant Mitchell, and how he'd have dealt with the Daleks and so on, 'the slags', and this approach, coupled with the genuinely nightmarish storylines the writers came up with did, I think, bring something new to the series. As well, in the end, and perhaps inevitably, as something rather old, the blazing return of Russell, who appeared on set at the end-of-shoot party, announcing he was there to save the day.

'Good luck with that mate,' I said, hiding behind a robot as Stephen Fry's larger, camper, younger brother came stamping down the corridor, into the sort of creaking, Gothic scenery the show hadn't seen since the mid-to-late Seventies, when Mary Whitehouse would file a weekly complaint.

'Look at this place! It's like bloody *Alien* in here! What have you done to my beautiful programme?' Russell shouted, looking deranged in the sickly green lighting, although cutting a dash in his broad-brimmed hat and turquoise darts shirt combination, his scarf trailing the floor. 'This is your fault, Mitchell! Well, yours and Stephen's. Where is he anyway?'

'The Thirtieth century,' I said, 'or the gents. Which do you think?'

'My God,' hissed Russell, as, safe behind the automaton, I continued the almost hourly quest for the perfect line. 'I bloody knew this was going to happen . . . I can see,' he continued, with an air of manifest destiny, 'that I'm going to have to step up to the plate.'

'Right,' I said, 'is that for lunch, or dinner?'

As befits a traveller of time and space, I think I saw stars for about an hour after that. He packs quite a punch, does the Welshman.

Last things then. Well, it was an open secret on the show that Russell had long had his eye on the keys to the Tardis, and here he was now, with the BBC over a barrel after the rumours about the drugs on set, and, in particular, the reviews of the new Doctor's exploits, from which, it was said, the living room furniture offered no real refuge. And then there were the ratings, and the hundreds of calls, and the thousands of e-mails, from outraged parents. It became clear, fairly quickly, that the new series was the sort of faux-pas that Broadcasting House couldn't really afford. Which left Russell perfectly placed to return to the show like a conquering hero, while tabling a list of what, under any other circumstances, might have been considered unreasonable demands. So that's basically what he did. Twirling his floor-length scarf, no doubt, as he plotted my Doctor's early death. He left a few messages on my answer phone actually, explaining not just what was going to happen to my character, but why, because of the bag on his head, my presence on set would not be required.

The transformation scene was quite something. Left for dead in the sewers of Mars, the Doctor's body suddenly balloons . . . .

So had Russell seen all this coming when he'd agreed to cast me? Had he planned, all along for this to happen? In short, had I been played by a, if not *the*, Master? *Who* fans can be wankers about that, I guess.

Still, he's welcome to the thing. As much as anything else, your time in the role is defined by who follows you (everyone usually prefers the prior incarnation) so considering what Russell's up to now, sailing through time and space like a fluorescent Welsh whale, as if he's swallowed all twelve of the previous Doctors, I'm not ruling out a future critical U-turn. Then again, I'm a timelord no longer, so I'll just have to wait and see, I suppose. Like all the other civilians.

So in the meantime, what can I tell you? That if you happen to run into me on the convention circuit, where I imagine I'll be spending a fair bit of time, and you're a fan of my series, and not the other sort of fan, the kind that's vocal on the internet, these days –

'Matt Mitchell is a fucking wanker! You be the gayest doctor ever, blood!' etcetera (I suppose I shouldn't look) then I'll be over at the bar, basically.

Signing autographs, and maybe one day, eventually, if the stars align, the calendar, the posters, and the DVDs. The series has it's critics, for sure, but shit on them.

LARRY TROTTER AND THE STAFF OF POWER

Perhaps the first thing to say is that I have read the books. All of them, from cover to cover. It isn't something I'd have chosen to do, necessarily, because as Mr Lawrence 'Larry' Trotter, and a practising magician myself (not the Paul Daniels kind) I'd been more or less plagued by the jokes for years. Plus, as a gentleman of a certain vintage, I'd always felt that to be seen with a Potter, at least in public, would be to run the risk of being labelled a potential sex offender. Which, as a student of the occult, is about the last thing you need. Any more speculation.

Still, by the time I found myself detained, for a couple of months, in the kind of facility I wouldn't recommend (in spite of what sometimes said in The Daily Mail, it isn't like a hotel) that ship had already sailed. And there isn't a lot else to do in jail, except for possibly heroin – at the age of fifty five, I was too old for sodomy, the gym or adult education, and by about week four, I'd almost exhausted the prison library. There's only so many times you can re-read *The Ballad Of Reading Gaol*, after all, or the complete works of Dan Brown. So at that point, with a certain grim symmetry, and in spite of the comments from the lads on my wing, the Potters had beckoned.

And actually, they weren't all that bad. The first couple of books weren't really my thing, being perhaps a bit childish. I'll be coming back to this later, but essentially, I'd never wanted children. In any shape, form or description. However, by *The Prisoner Of Azkaban*, ironically enough, I was more or less hooked on Harry's adventures. On his struggles with authorities (the press, the schools, the government and so on) that seem almost wilfully blind to his gifts as a sorcerer. In fact, you could almost say I identified.

With hindsight, then, I could have been more discreet about my magical practice, especially round the office. Perhaps if I had been, I could have avoided a degree of unpleasantness, in the tabloids particularly, in which, it appeared, I had been sent down from the court of public opinion as a monster, a paedophile and a diabolist, before my case reached trial.

Admittedly, it hadn't helped that I'd been arrested in a hooded top, or cowl, if you'd rather, in one of the government's new build academies. Or that underneath, as the ritual required, I was sky clad (that's naked to the layman, and sadly, the police) except for some piercings, daubs and shamanic tattoos. Nor was it ideal that I'd been interrupted by security while chalking a pentagram on the gymnasium floor. Or, that as a senior partner at a top City law firm, where I suppose I'd felt indestructible, I'd been openly talking about my beliefs for a number of years, This, as a revelation, was like catnip to the red-tops. They love a good Satanist, those guys. Not that I actually was a Satanist. But you try explaining that, if trapped, with your arse out in the midst of a faith school. Under the circumstances, even I, as a solicitor of some distinction, was at something of a loss as to how to defend myself. The pressure to file a plea of insanity was strong, at times.

Still, as a fifty-something guy, and a childless bachelor (avoid arrestable offences, if this is on your CV – they really don't like it) I had made enough money. And eventually, you have to make a stand, for what you believe in. Plus three months inside, even on the beast's wing, which actually isn't all that bad (as a middle-aged man, how much danger are you really in, as long as you're careful at meal times? You aren't exactly much of a target, after all, as long as you stay out of Gen Pop) had to beat being submitted for psychiatric evaluation. Which could, quite conceivably, have gone on indefinitely.

'But you don't understand. There are more things in heaven and earth . . .'

'No mate, there aren't.' This from some guy who may well have earned his Masters in human psychology while studying under doctors Duck and Mouse at a red brick ex-polytechnic. If you can avoid this, you should.

So, I should explain about the ritual. Or perhaps I shouldn't, but here goes anyway. Just before my incarceration, I'd been experimenting with a more freestyle approach to my occult practice. In particular, with the idea of the shamanic vision quest, as applied to an urban context. This involves putting yourself in an altered state, either through meditation, or the illicit, but frankly more convenient, use of LSD, sacred mushrooms, and so on, then trailing the signs and portents across the city on public transport (driving, for obvious reasons, isn't really an option) until you arrive at a point of revelation. This doesn't always work. You can end up shitting yourself in Hackney or somewhere, in Peckham, or the Isle of Dogs, with nothing but an expensive cab ride, or more likely, a hellish two hour trip on the night bus back home to show for your trouble. So I'm not saying that I'd mastered the technique, being much more comfortable with raising the Great God Pan, or related, from the safety of the converted church I owned in Highgate – again, that wasn't something the press really liked.

Anyway – long story short – after a strange afternoon,

when, I suppose frustrated by my lack of success with this so far, I'd doubled the dose, and consequently spent what felt like years on the underground, trying, like one of the Biblical three wise men, to navigate the tube map as if the stations were stars. Until I wound up in Clapham, outside a freshly-built London faith academy. Which, lit up like a flat-pack, Ikea cathedral, seemed to throb with a source of mystical power, hidden somewhere inside. What was in there? A stone from a standing circle? A branch from a holy tree? Who knew where the developers had sourced their materials?

Anything seemed possible, as, at this point, an angel of the Lord, the angel Gabriel actually, appeared above the building. And informed me that there was something in there that I had to retrieve a rod, a sceptre or something like that, or something bad was going to happen. Well, paging Dr Freud, I know – I had been single for quite some time. Equally, though, it's hard to argue with divine intervention. As a student of the occult, I'd seen some strange things in my time, since around about the time of ex-wife's departure, twenty years earlier, but this was unprecedented. Fifty foot high and crackling with energy, the angel Gabriel seemed like quite a result. Except, of course, that you actually have to think about doing what he wants. Which, in this case anyway, was a little bit vague. I had to get the staff, yes, but where was it? What did it look like?

It was time to go home and some research. Which involved crystal balls, crystal meth and conversations with spirits, angels, demons, and so on – you have to hedge your bets. The occult is not a precise science. Performing a ritual's a bit like following a recipe, but interpreting the results is more like tasting a dish in an unknown cuisine, and trying to guess the ingredients. Which I hadn't made an especially good fist of. So it was back to the school with my gym kit, you could say, with the uniform on and an unholy back-pack. Damn it, basically.

So, six months later, fresh out of prison, struck off in grand style from the company's pension scheme, but still undaunted, I was waiting in line for the debut performance of the school's Nativity play. Since I'd last visited, getting into the place had become more difficult, and not just in terms of the exam passes necessary. Security, never that lax when I'd first broken in, had been stepped up to the point where ID was required, and possibly a bag search. All in all, it was like going through customs. There was a fifteen foot fence surrounding the playground, topped with razor wire, and a sign that mentioned guards with attack dogs, Tasers and so forth, patrolling the hallways and the grounds after dark. Well, I only had myself to blame. But, on the other hand, were the new measures working entirely against me? What were ordinary families meant to think about a school, after all, that had taken on the aspect of a gated community? Not much, it seemed. Because of accusations in the press that the academies were elitist, and draining resources from the local comps, the board of governors had been forced to open the performance to the general public, so prospective parents from the community could see that the place was open to anyone. And not just a private school, by any other name, for middle class parents with careers in the arts, who expected the state to pick up after them. As a top rate tax payer who'd been vilified in the liberal press, just as much as by the tabloids, if more for my job than the alleged devil worship, I wasn't in the mood to let little Portia or Tony off the hook, any more that I was little Deshawn or Tarzan.

I don't know if you've ever been in a car crash, that feeling of almost watching, in slow motion, as everything seems to crumple around you. Drugs, black magic and a job in the City, to say nothing of prison, and the Potter novels, had, quite conceivably, driven me mad, but there didn't seem to be much I could do about it now.

So, would my disguise hold up? In any great enterprise, there will be moments of doubt, I told myself, as I moved closer to the end of the line. In a fleece top, glasses and polo shirt combo, with a freshly-shaved head, I looked indistinguishable from most of the dads – it's true that the clippers take ten years off. But, equally, I was minus a push chair, or a long-suffering partner. And, because I was going to have to perform the ritual again, what I had in my back-pack didn't really bear thinking about. This stuff isn't easy. The eye of a newt, or the wing of a bat, just isn't going to cut it. For the right kind of material, you need to think about graveyards, and the waste bins outside of emergency rooms. I could see the dads, the ex-ravers, the Arsenal fans, beginning to sense a traitor in their midst.

'Mr . . . Foster?' said the bouncer, flipping his way through my box fresh credentials – who says you can't make friends in prison? 'How you doing this evening?'

'Good. Yourself?'

'Great. You're here on your own, yeah?'

'Yes. My . . . wife is in hospital.'

'Expecting, is she?'

'I should be so lucky! No, mate, she's a nurse.'

'I see. Shall we do a quick check anyway? I dunno if you're aware of this, but a nutter broke in during the summer.'

'Really? A nutter? No, I didn't know . . . maybe my lad shouldn't go to this school after all?'

'Whatever. Can you confirm your address, sir?'

'Sorry, is there a problem?'

'Not if you don't make one. Where do you live?'

Say what you like about Paedo Phil, (who doesn't like to be called that) but he does cook up a mean fake ID.

'Okay,' the guard grunted, 'In you go, Mr Foster. Enjoy.'

'Thank you. I'm going to have to go to the toilet, though.'

142

'The toilet?' said the bouncer.

'I have some business at attend to.'

'Mr Foster, I don't want to know.'

And how right he was. Cutting my arm up in one of the cubicles, so this time I could draw a proper pentagram (chalk was one of the reasons I'd gone wrong last time, it seemed) I did find myself questioning the rationality of my actions.

'Lord,' I muttered, 'let this burden pass from me.'

'Know the feeling, mate,' said a voice from next door. 'Still, better out than in. Is one of your kiddies performing?'

'I can't talk about that now.'

'Vindaloo, was it? I feel your pain. Hope you won't be sitting next to me, anyway!'

'I'm sure I won't be.'

'I don't like your tone, mate,' he said. 'You've got an accent. Do you write for the papers?'

'Gabriel?' I said. '*Gabriel?*'

'Yes Larry?' the angel sighed, emerging, incandescent, from the enchanted, blood-stained toilet, 'You called?'

'Make him go away.'

'But why, Larry? Why should I?'

'Okay, I'll do what you want.'

'Finally . . .'

'I just don't know what it is.'

'Well then, let's go through it, one more time . . .'

'Right,' I said, after the explanation, the voice now silenced. 'But there are cameras everywhere.'

'And?'

'Gabriel, if the kid playing Joseph puts up a struggle, I'm totally fucked.'

'Larry, if you can't put your faith in an angel, who are you going to trust?'

'Well, I . . .'

'Look, just get on with it. Bad things, need I remind you, are going to happen if you don't.'

'But what *bad things*? You've been vague about this.'

'I'm comparing you to Jesus in no other way, Larry. But like him, you're going to have to suck it up.'

'And that worked out so well . . .'

'You don't know what it would have been like if it hadn't been for the lad, Larry. He gets a bad press, it's true, but . . .'

'I know that feeling . . .'

'And that's why you were chosen, Larry, to wield the staff of power . . . seriously, stop fucking about.'

In the crit in the local paper, which praised the efforts of the cast, the reviewer couldn't help but note that the performance was somewhat soured by the hooded man who leapt on stage as the child was born and the angels descended (the clip's on YouTube) and wrestled Joseph's crook away from him. Yelling something about 'the prophecy', before seeming to vanish into the wings.

The police are questioning 'large, older men, with a possible interest in fetish subculture'. The academy has apologised to the parents of the cast, and has promised to step up its security measures, when it reopens, in the New Year.

But will there be a New Year? I wonder. They saw the lot, I suppose, but how dare they call me fat?

THE H-MEISTER HITS THIRTY

Twenty seven, then. It isn't quite the big Three Oh, things aren't that bad, yet, but equally, that red-ringed sign on the highway of life seems around the next bend. And there are no U-turns possible, no appeals to the traffic cops – you can't just flash your ID at the Fates, sadly, if there's some sort of problem. It can be a turbulent time in a chap's life. Better men than me, Kurt Cobain, for example, have at this point decided to cash in their chips. Admittedly Cobain, by all accounts, had his fit of the vapours because of hassles with his filly, and because everyone around him just expected too much – as a prince of the realm with no totty to speak of, I was more at the other end of the spectrum. Since the end of my army career, or possibly before then, no one, it seemed had expected very much from the H-Meister, at all.

So I suppose it depends what's a chap had been up to, all this time, But if it looks, to the untrained eye, as if all he's been doing is having a wild, crazy time in Whisky Mist, Boujis and in some ways the military, between busts in the red-tops for the occasional gaff on the political front – contrary to what's been said in the papers, Dad and Grandpa Phil really do appear to be in the genes – then it's probably time for a couple of changes.

Time to slow down at parties, and speed up at work . . . well, 'work', I know, but you get the idea. Time to abandon those rock and roll dreams. Time to think about marriage, one's health and one's future. Time to develop a couple of interests – charity; the environment; underprivileged kids. Time to stop thinking about throwing in the towel with a grand, final gesture, one a chap, in the end, will never get round to making, so time, in other words, to start trying to think about the next royal wedding.

I'd never particularly liked the sound of all this. As a veteran of bollockings from the bods at Buck house, I'd been hearing it for years. 'Sort yourself out, Bluff Prince', all that. 'You don't want to end up like Uncle Andrew.' Or, if I'd managed to slip up especially royally, 'Uncle Edward'. This last, in particular, was a bit of a grim spectre to raise.

Still, I don't suppose the trouble really started until my brother's big day.

Well, we've all seen it, I guess. Even the most avowed anti-monarchist can hardly have missed it. The wedding itself, or the commentary next morning.

Can I take a moment here to say how pleased I am about recent developments in the Murdoch empire? I gather the Dirty Digger's now considered 'unfit to run a newspaper'. Some of us have been saying that for ages, of course (presumably, the Murdoch ancestors were shipped off to the Antipodes for a reason in the first place) but equally, it's nice, as a British royal, to be considered right about something. It doesn't happen very often.

Anyway in the press next day (and I wish I could say it was only the tabloids,) I'd been accused, during the ceremony, of lingering over the spectacle that was Pippa Middleton's bottom. Well, hands in the air, it was fine arse, possibly even a world-beating bum. But while it was perfectly acceptable for the red-tops to drool, and for Joe Public to set up page after page on Facebook about it, for the H-Meister to make a jovial, off-the-cuff comment about the best man's duties with regard to the maid of honour . . . suddenly, everyone thinks you're Russell Brand, or somebody. A crazed, ginger sex pest.

Being blown out is one thing – we've all been there, I guess – but who needs it to read about it over their cornflakes? Third in line to the throne though I might be, I do still have feelings. It was in *The Mail*, it was in *The Guardian* . . . the list went on. Shares in the H-Meister PLC more or less plummeted after that. My name was mud on the debutante circuit. However much I tried to keep my gaze focused on the bar, it was backs to the wall when I walked into Boujis, the fillies now convinced, it seemed, that I was some kind of pervert, perhaps even the sort of chap who actively favours the tradesman's entrance. And if it's been decided that a bum's being stared at, how do you persuade the owner otherwise? I took to wearing my Ray Bans indoors, after dark, like George Michael or someone, but even that didn't work. In fact, it only seemed to make matters worse.

So, for the first time in my life perhaps, I began to feel the weight of loneliness. Wills wasn't around to hit the clubs with any more, he was too busy pressing the flesh in the colonies, plus even before 'Bumgate', as I've come to think of it, I'd never particularly got on with his bird. For a member of the public, that is, the enemy, and I'm afraid that's how I'm always going to see her, she has quite a bit to say for herself. If Buck House was *Big Brother*, (and in some ways it is, a real life soap full of odd individuals, more or less trapped under public scrutiny) I'd say she has a game plan. She talks about Mum a fair bit, for example, her and the Queen Mum, in the apparent belief that there's some sort of vacancy in the public's affections. That and all the children she's planning on having, each one moving the H-Meister further down the line of succession. As if anyone who knows anything about what's involved (The ceremonial state visits to Fiji and so on – for understandable reasons, the dancers more or less moon you for hours at a time, and not in a good way either) would want to be any closer to the throne than they already are. Try explaining this to La Middleton though, as I did last Christmas, and she tends to fix a chap with a rather gimlet eye.

'Why don't you just have another drink, Harry?' she said, once I finished my speech.

'Yeah, I should oil the old tonsils. I might smoke a fine cigar also.'

'Oh God, do you have to?'

'Yes, must you, Harry?' asked Grandmother.

'Out on the terrace, obviously.' I said. 'I'm not a complete monster.'

'Oh really?' said La Middleton.

'Yes, really.'

'Oh let the boy smoke his cigar.' Grandpa Phil interjected. 'What are they, Cuban?'

'More Columbian, I gather. But a lot of, err, love has been put into them, apparently.'

'Rolled on the thighs of dusky maidens, eh? Jolly good.'

'Now Philip,' said the Queen, 'remember your heart.'

'Cabbage, I am ninety one years old. I'm not going to join the lad. But it is Christmas, after all. Where's the harm?'

The QE2 had seen her speech on TV a bit too recently to put up much of a struggle, it seemed.

So I lit up. With every puff though, as the thick, scented fog descended on the garden, I began to see, ever more clearly, how things at the Palace might develop, in time. With everyone else in the drawing room basically, while the H-Meister kept his lonely vigil out on the lawn. What changes might La Middleton be plotting on making, once the throne was hers? A reduced civil list? Buck House open to the lifestyle section of *The Mail On Sunday*? Ramblers loose on the Highland estate? The H-Meister packed off on increasingly drawn-out fact-finding trips to Kazakhstan or the Falklands, ostensibly there to promote British business? It all seemed on the cards, and would Wills, who was out of the room at the time, be able to stop her? He's a great bloke, my bro, but, crowned king though he may be, will he be also wearing the trousers?

Still, these were standard reservations. Nobody really likes it where their drinking pals get hitched, especially not to 'I love you, now change!' types like La Middleton. And tensions between a new bride and an errant best man are almost in the script somewhere. Plus God knew what Rafe (who, bless him, is unlikely to marry any time soon) had laced the cigar with. Not skunk, I'd been clear about that, but opium possibly? A bit of cocaine? The room-clearing fug of a fine Montecristo can cover over a multitude of sins. So maybe I was being a bit paranoid. But if so, I wasn't the only one. Between you, me and the fencepost, the QE2 seemed rather nervous at meals that Christmas. I'm not saying the kitchen hired extra security, but there was a bit of an atmosphere when La Middleton insisted on raiding the fridge without Cook's help.

Anyway, I digress. The point is that since Bumgate, the old social calendar had taken a bit of a hiding. All the old war horses had left for the country, or got serious jobs, or worse still, fiancés, and there was a new generation at Whisky Mist. On the packed, sweaty dance floors I'd once felt at home on, I now felt a bit like the bloke in *How Soon Is Now*. 'You go and you stand on your own, then you leave on your own,' and so on. I'd never been all that much of a Smiths fan. 'Cheer up guys,' I used to think, 'it may never happen'. But now I began to see merit in even Morrissey's solo albums. Long walks were taken, alone in the rain. On occasion, late at night, after ten or so gins, I even tried my hand at poetry. Basically, thoughts of mortality began to creep in. I was nearly thirty, and what had I achieved? What was I ever going to achieve? And say what you like about my brother's big day (and I would probably agree with at least some of it anyway) it was quite an event. All in all, it seemed like handy karma if I had one of my own. Because how else, realistically, was I going to be able to put Bumgate behind me?

So I set up an account on Match.com, but no one was interested. I couldn't believe this either, so I tried Cupid.com, and various others. I even logged on to some of the more risqué sites, Sexbook and so on, or whatever it's called, but to no avail. I poured my heart out about what I wanted from a filly, but unless you post a photo, which I couldn't really do, on-line dating is bit of a bust. Eventually, at a low ebb, I gave an interview to one of the papers (I can't remember which . . . all right, it probably was *The Sun*) about how much it sucked to be a lonesome prince.

That was when Channel 4 got in touch.

They didn't, they said, like to think of the H-Meister being on his tod, and especially not with the Jubilee coming up, never mind the Olympics.

'Right,' I said, 'but what are you going to do about it? Fix me up?'

As it turned out, this was exactly what they wanted to do.

'Right . . .' I said. 'But what might this involve?'

Well it all seemed to hinge on the final of the Men's 100 Metres, and whether I had tickets.

'Yeah, I'm sitting next to Elton John actually, with an empty chair, so far, on the right . . . I'm not all that happy about it . . . he's virtually a member of the family, that bloke.'

But this was great, C4 thought. Their idea was a Jubilee version of *Celebrity Blind Date*, with a seat by yours truly, at the Games' most popular event, as the grand prize.

'Really?' I said. 'I was actually thinking of phoning in sick. I'm not all that keen on athletics, to be honest. Plus, if you ask Sir Elton to get his round in, it's like being caught bumming one of the corgis . . .'

'Right . . .' said C4. Still, as they pointed out, the race would be over in less than ten seconds.

'That's true,' I said, perking up a bit. 'I hadn't thought of it that way. And then me and my date would have a night out afterwards, I suppose?'

Absolutely, was the word. C4 also said that because the quality of the date, they were expecting top drawer entrants.

'Thanks guys,' I said, quite touched, until they reminded me of the show's format, in which, per force, the H-Meister would be a mystery contestant.

So you're supposed to run this stuff past the Palace. You can't just show up on telly and make a fool of yourself without warning everyone, is the protocol. Uncle Edward's *It's A Royal Knockout* is still a bit of a sqoodge-covered elephant in the drawing room, as it were, at family reunions. Along with Mum's telly interview, when she spilled the beans finally, (and, to be fair, my SS uniform thing) it's to this day considered a major faux-pas, one of the darker events in recent family history, before the Palace PR machine, as we know it these days, really got into gear.

On the other hand though, during the plans for the Diamond Jube, there'd been an awkward meeting about one of the photo shoots.

'Look, guys, after that fuss at the wedding, I don't really think I should stand behind her.'

'This is how we feel too.'

'But is it a problem? She can pose on the other side, can't she? Or I can, or whatever.'

'The photographer doesn't think so. It's a question of composition, you see.'

'Yeah, I did study art . . . okay then, I suppose it isn't that big a deal. I'll stand behind her if that's what it takes.'

'But this is the point. Pippa feels uncomfortable . . .'

'Oh does she? All right, I get it. But if it's the rear of the year or the H-Meister, then it's no competition, surely?'

And as it turned out, it wasn't.

Was I still smarting a bit, rather in the manner of a smacked arse, in fact, from the Palace's decision? I think I may have been. Were there movements afoot to sideline the H-Meister? Possibly from the Middleton end? Well, who knew, but it had been quite a while since I'd last done something to outrage the Palace, or the papers, I guess – perhaps a last hurrah was in order? Between the pair of them, after all, Buck House and the red-tops had more or less conspired to finish off Mum, so 'what the hell?', in effect, was the long and the short of my thinking, as I said yes to C4.

To what I should have remembered, but didn't, had long been the home of the Alternative Queen's speech.

I should say, to begin with, that I didn't know it would be broadcast during the Jubilee. It was in the contract, I suppose, but who reads that stuff? Not I, I fear. Nor did I realise that someone called Alan Carr would be doing the honours, and not Cilla Black.

Who is this character? Is he famous? Is anyone familiar with his work? He seems a bit of a loose cannon. Five minutes into the show, and the Middleton bottom had already been raised about eight times. Carr looked to be a sort of a court jester type. You have to pretend to be a good sport about this stuff, the Fool speaking truth to the palace and such, especially in front of a live TV audience, but no wonder these characters used to be executed, I found myself thinking, more than once.

'So, I'm all of a flutter,' was Carr's opening gambit. 'What a hunk, eh viewers? I've always fancied being taken up the aisle by a handsome young prince!'

'I ah . . .' I began.

'Well, you wouldn't be doing this show if you weren't

desperate, would you love?'

'Evidently not . . .'

'Still, don't you worry, your Uncle Alan understands! Just think of me as your fairy Godmother! Now we have some fine princesses lined up for you this evening . . . in fact you could even say that they're queen material!'

'Oh God,' I remember thinking, already sweating profusely, 'how many of these are trannies? Not all of them surely?'

And that, dear reader, is about the last thought I clearly recall. Sitting there under the studio lights, on a pink and bling set that seemed excessively camp (as us royals are now, I supposed) I sort of shut down mentally, when the scale of what I'd agreed to became apparent. I'm not even sure about the questions I asked, the C4 boffins, once they'd seen my suggestions, having written them for me. Plus I'd got a bit tanked up in hospitality beforehand. So the show's now really just a blur of innuendo. About, say, my army career.

'I did serve my country, Alan.'

'And was it good for the country? Did Britain scream with abandonment? Or did it just lie back and think of England?' And so on.

At times, it was as much as I could do not to demonstrate a bit of the old combat training.

The *Blind Date* format used to be simple enough. As the chap doing the choosing, you'd pitch your questions so as to establish which of the contestants was most simpatico, when it came to the matter of a roll in the hay. Well, fair enough, anyone could follow that. But now black was white, and up was down, because if I didn't want to end up attending the Olympics with a bloke in a dress (and it's not that I'm prejudiced, but I didn't, really) I had to develop a bit of a strategy. It went against every fibre of my being, but the more risqué the answers the fillies came up with, the more I had to reject them, it seemed, on pain of a drubbing in next day's papers. 'Bluff Prince Hal And The Fairytale . . . Prince?' As a veteran of these things, it would have been a bit tricky. So I had to go with whoever sounded the *least* likely to subject the H-Meister to various unchristian sexual practices. For whoever seemed the most diffident, or subdued. Accordingly, long story short, number three, Delilah from Hackney, was who I picked, in the end.

'Are you sure you don't want to go for number two?'

'No, I, ah, went before I came on stage, Alan.'

'Look, I do the jokes here!'

'That's debatable, Alan.'

'Now we've got on so well, oh Bluff Prince! Let's not spoil it now!'

The screen rearranged itself. The moment was here. It seemed inconceivable that none of the contestants had actually twigged who was asking the questions, but it looked like C4 had been as good as their word, when they said they'd guard it like a military secret. Or actually, a bit closer than that. Certainly much closer than anyone had bothered to do about my location in Afghanistan, that time.

Anyway, contestant one, Camilla of the husky voice, was, as suspected, a bit of a drag queen. She seemed nice enough, but was the ghost of Uncle Edward, of royal slip-ups past, floating over the stage as Camilla exited? Perhaps talking to plants in an SS uniform? I'd say so, yeah. Carr was gutted, I could tell, the headlines might have been massive, and in a way, I was sorry to disappoint. But equally, Camilla? Did C4 think I was totally nuts? Probably best not to go there, really.

Contestant two, on the other hand, was a serious stunner. The kind of filly who'd drag a chap into sin, break his heart into pieces then sell the story to everyone. Buck House has a history with this sort of totty, and it never ends well, but still, what a mover, I thought, as she swept off gently into the wings. I suppose the old tongue was lolling out rather.

'Ooh, nice bum!' Alan said. 'I did say, didn't I?'

'I'm happy with my decision, Alan.' I choked.

'So, number three!'

Number three, Delilah, was, is, a single mum from a council estate. Channel Four go at you like that. But equally, she does have mysterious grace. I've seen a bit of her already and we get on quite well. She likes the odd curry, and going clubbing and so on. She enjoys nights out in pubs where this isn't this pressure to stand on ceremony, because the red-tops aren't usually waiting the pavement outside, at least unless there's a riot. And actually everyone's been pretty welcoming. Just get the ales in and you're fine, it seems. Even the bodyguards are okay about this.

'It's good,' Ron, my head of security said the other evening, 'to know we can get into a proper ruck, if any mug tries it on.'

Basically, Delilah has shown me a different world, one I never really knew existed. You see this stuff on telly, of course, but still ... I had, for example, never been to a Harvester before.

In Nandos (so exotic!) the other day, I mentioned something about my burgeoning feelings.

'Look mate,' she said, over the hot wings, 'I ain't easy, if that's what you're thinking.'

'No, but you seem so much more ... broad-minded than the fillies in Boujis.'

'Don't get your hopes up, boy,' she said, but tellingly, I think, she didn't leave the restaurant, or throw her Tango in my face.

And our family backgrounds aren't entirely dissimilar. She comes from a long line of what might be considered British eccentrics – divorces abound, and some of her uncles have been on benefits for decades. Plus finding a seat for her son, little Elton, at the Men's 100 metres final, means the boy's namesake will have to move to a chair further back in the stadium. In a way, I could marry her for that alone.

The Palace don't like any of this, of course, but what can they do? Stock in the the H-Meister PLC has never been higher. I'd never do anything to appease the red-tops, it's true, but equally, all past sins look to melt away somehow, when I'm papped in the park with little Elton, sending him sailing round on the swings, Delilah, the proud mum, looking on in the background, Bumgate, now a distant memory.

It's a question, I guess, of what I could do next. As discussed, I'm not getting any younger. So am I, if she'll have me, going to walk up the aisle in Westminster Abbey, with little Elton in a pushchair, ready to marry the lovely Delilah? As a plan, it has definite fairytale, Merry England qualities. Or so Max Clifford, who's already left a few messages on my mobile (no good wondering how he got the number, I suppose) seems to think. That I could be sort of a Chav Bluff royal, a true people's prince. I'm already half way there apparently. I'm obviously not going to ring the bloke back, but, does he have a point?

Honestly, I don't know. It may not be a love match exactly, but these things rarely are, and it would be one where it hurts for the Palace, at least. As well, ironically perhaps, for the Middleton faction. After all, what could Kate say about Delilah, at least in public, without running the risk of alienating the everyday, red-top-reading, salt of the earth punters that she appears, at the moment, to be keen on impressing? So there is that.

Plus, the one thing you do have to do, as a British royal, is get married. This is drummed into you quite early on, that the UK taxpayer will put up with almost anything, in terms of far-out behaviour, as long as you give them this one special day. I suppose even I can't really argue with that.

LAVENDER BUNNY AND THE GROUCHO CLUB

So it was dark, it was cold and it was raining heavily, 'like God himself is weeping on Soho, Mike, weeping, or worse', as we made our way out of the Pillars of Hercules.

'Mike,' said LB, who I'd taken to carrying around with me most of the time, in the same way as glamour models who've totally lost it do with their Chihuahuas, or Yorkshire terriers, 'I think we should get a taxi.'

'There could be a problem with that, LB.'

'What problem? Mike, we must arrive looking stylish. We have to make a grand entrance. Parsons is going to be there, after all. And possibly Self. And maybe even Burchill.'

'Yeah ...' I said, viewing the prospect with some trepidation, hence the six pints of Stella I'd just imbibed. Veterans of the Groucho Club, Will Self, Julie Burchill and Tony Parsons, notorious, in Self's case anyway, for their biting wit, had recently said some ... unkind things in the press about the new novel, *Man Flu*. *Man Flu*, that was, which was potentially up for an award this evening.

'LB, what do we care for these baubles and trinkets? I am a serious artist.'

'Of course you are Mike. Of course you are. But we

care about these baubles and trinkets because they help shift units. Plus, Parsons is going to think you're a lightweight if you don't show up. He more or less called you a shit house on Twitter, Mike. Are you going to let him get away with that? When he no doubt thinks *his* new book is the dog's bollocks.'

'Well, he's half right.'

'That's the spirit!'

I waved down a cab.

'Where to, mate?' said the driver.

'Dean Street.'

'Where in Dean Street?'

'We're going to the Groucho!' said LB (oh, how his little heart seemed to thrill to the sound – he was always a bit of a star fucker), 'For the ceremony!'

'Are you taking the piss, son?'

'According to Parsons, Burchill and Self (it sounds like a law firm, don't it?)' said LB, 'Mike is!'

'Right. Well according to me, mate, the Groucho Club, from here, is about a three minute walk away.'

'But the weather's inclement,' LB said, 'Oh son of the oil. Plus a three minute walk may not be within Mike's powers.'

'Seriously?'

'I've had a couple of morale boosters.'

'All right then,' sighed the driver. 'Hop in.'

'Mate,' he continued after a minute or so, eyeing us in the rear view mirror, 'I know you, don't I?'

'I'll pay for all the damages . . .'

No, it's not that. I saw you on Jonathan Ross the other week, and you looked in bother, mate. All right, there's form for this, Rod Hull and that. But what your . . . friend said went further than Emu grabbing Michael Parkinson in the cods.'

'But Ross does a lot of work for charity.' said LB, 'Just like Jimmy Savile used to. Was it so wrong for me to join the dots?'

'Yeah, it was. It looked like he wanted to punch your lights out.'

'I wanted to punch Ross's lights out too. He isn't as funny as he thinks he is . . .' muttered LB.

'You used to be a laugh as well, mate. Me and the missus, we voted for you on Big Brother . . . and look at the state of you now.'

'No, it's a cold, honestly . . . too many late nights, I guess. That's what my girlfriend says anyway,' I laughed, brokenly.

'You wanna lay off the nosebag, son'

'It's under control.' I said, trying to appease the guy, slipping him ten quid for a three minute journey, before, admittedly, rushing down the alleyway behind the Groucho to do a line off the top of the nearest wheelie bin. And in the rain as well.

LB, meanwhile, was floating about in the twilight of the back street. Since, after the incident the Christmas before, when we'd astrally journeyed to Hell by accident that time, he didn't need to be physically present for me to see him. But he'd always wanted to go to the Groucho, it was his Mecca, in a way, so I couldn't very well have left him at home. He'd have been so disappointed if I had. No good deed, however, goes unpunished.

'Mike,' he said, 'You should have taken a swing at that person.'

'What, the driver?'

'Yes.'

'But LB, he might have phoned the tabloids. Or worse still, the Times Literary Supplement.'

'Mike, I want you to listen, because this is very important. You have to try and keep things together this evening.'

'But how am I expected to do that? I can't deal with celebrities . . . what if I run into Lenny Henry or someone, and end up congratulating him on his work?'

'If that happens, Mike, you probably won't remember it next day.'

'Yeah, but he might.'

'Mike,' said LB, who'd been a lot more vocal and assertive, more of an alpha male really, since we'd got back from Hell, 'On this journey we've been on, what do I always tell you, even in our darkest hours?'

'Crush our enemies?'

'Crush our enemies.'

LB and I had been to The Pillars Of Hercules for some time, prior to this exchange. Was he just a morbid hallucination? And was I, like a fashionista on too much coke, on too much coke? Earlier that day, my therapist, Dr Judy ('Dr Shit', as LB described her) who I'd commissioned after the nth case of writer's block, had said as much. That I had to at least begin to accept the idea that Lavender Bunny was a way of 'acting out' my feelings of rage and impotence. Mainly impotence.

In response to this LB had pointed out that Dr Judy hadn't been on television, whereas he and I had.

'Big Bother, Celebrity Come Dine With Me – argue with that, if you think you can, Dr Shit!'

'I actually have been a panellist on Big Brother, Lavender Bunny. I know who you are.'

'Oh.'

'It is good, Michael,' Dr Judy continued, 'That you feel your . . . friend can be a part of this process. However he is, I think, at the heart of your problems. Which seem many, and very serious. We've got a lot of work ahead of us . . .'

'Have we?'

'We do. And these sessions will remain unproductive if you are unwilling to embrace them without recourse to what, frankly, appears to be a psychological crutch.'

'I told you you should have rung up an escort agency instead, Mike.'

So it had already been a long afternoon. For months, years even, in the writing game, nothing much happens, you're just sitting around at home, taking dictation from your imaginary friend, or muse, who is possibly also a demon from Hell. Does Salman Rushdie feel the same? I like to think so.

And then all of a sudden you get a call from your publisher, and it's time to go out there and . . . meet people, to press the flesh, because against all the odds, you've been put up as a contender for a literary prize.

I wasn't too sure what this award was about. Something to do with Male British writing, perhaps? Bloke Lit, in effect, a riposte to the Orange Prize? Novels for guys who don't usually read them? Football and divorce, geezer porn, basically, men behaving badly, that kind of thing? Certainly, we were up against Tony Parsons, along with five or six other guys who were scowling out of the promotional literature as if what we'd entered was a John McVicar lookalike contest.

So there'd been a slight detour along the way. Stumbling out of the Pillars of Hercules, as according to LB, Philip Larkin and others often had, I'd felt like we were walking sideways in the footsteps of genius.

I had no idea what to expect from the Groucho. Was it still the hot spot it had been in the Nineties, where the celebrities, comedians and cunts of the day had gone to let their hair down, away from the prying eyes of Joe and Joanne Public? Keith Allen emerging like Santa from the Gents ('Go Dasher, go Dancer . . . Go Donner and Blitzen!') the singer from Blur taking on a micro-skirted Jo Guest at pool, while Steve Coogan and Jarvis Cocker looked on from the side, taking notes, and various ad men and journos clogged up the bar? Or was everyone on the wagon in the Cotswolds these days, involved in some variation of raising children, or farming sheep? Or the other way round? Was Alex from Blur involved in some kind of death cult? Only time would tell.

Before LB and I had gone to Hell (I'd OD-ed in the bathtub, basically – it wasn't a dignified episode) there had been a real danger I was going to have to go back to the City, cap in hand, for, horrendously, less money than I'd been on before. Everyone laughing about my failed career, LB whispering constantly into my ear about the various ways in which the office coffee machine could be turned into an IED? It wouldn't have been ideal, so once we got back from the abyss, we'd come to an arrangement. That LB, who'd been a muse to Philip Larkin and James Dean, he said, was going to write the next book. Everything would be all right, he said, fame and riches would surely follow, as long as I did exactly what he told me,

Hence *Man Flu*. We were tapping into a feeling of post-Credit Crunch angst, was the plan. Mark, the narrator, is a City high flyer who's going through a mid-life crisis. Not because he dislikes the work – he's absolutely fine with the money and so on – but because there are moves afoot in the boardroom against him. There's a promotion coming up, but if he doesn't get it he's going to look like . . . a fool. But all his scheming leads nowhere, until finally, in a Hamlet moment, he hits the bar too hard at a client meet and greet and, after delivering an impassioned cri-de-coeur to his assembled colleagues, drops his trousers, and falls from grace. This, the first section, is entitled *Not In Front Of The Customers*.

And so begins his path to redemption. I hadn't, if I'm honest, been convinced about this. I was inclined to send Mark off into London's flesh pots, on a lost weekend or a voyage of discovery, from Knightsbridge to Limehouse, and into the Thames, but no, LB said.

'Mark isn't to do that if we want to sell books, Mike.'
'But LB . . .'

'No.'

The love interest, he said, wasn't to be a lap dancer Mark hooks up with in Babes of Mayfair, Candy or Bambi, say. Instead, she, Pauline, is an A&E nurse and a single mother, who Mark meets in Casualty, at four in the morning on the fateful evening, after disgracing himself in a number of further ways.

'No honestly, I walked into a lamp post.'

'Pull the other one, mate.'

'No really, I did . . . it seemed to leap out at me.'

So Mark, on the skids career-wise, is forced, after years of not showing up for weddings, parties or anything, to return to his parent's home in Dagenham, where he runs into Pauline again. While trying to court Pauline, with diminishing supplies of pills, cocaine and money (so he has to get wasted in the local, thus running into faces from the old days who are only too happy to see him on his uppers) Mark learns how hollow his materialism is, and about the value of roots, family and the ties of community. There are touching scenes involving Mark and Pauline's son, Wayne, having a kickabout and so on, Mark wheezing on the lawn like a wounded elephant as the kid run rings around him. To the point where, in a last ditch attempt to win Pauline over, he uses his financial skills to stop the local kids football pitch from being turned into Yuppie flats.

This had been a hard scene to write.

'LB, can't the developers win?'

'I'd like the bulldozers to come in too, Mike. The children realising, as the field is destroyed, that their dreams of the Premier League are now over, and they'll have to get jobs slinging rock instead.'

'Yeah!'

'We can't do it, Mike.'

'Why not?'

'Well Richard and Judy wouldn't like it.'

So in the end, of course, Mark saves the day and

'Reader, he marries her.'

It was 'bittersweet' and 'heart-warming', it was disgustingly cynical, but it was hard to argue with the rave reviews in the Mail On Sunday, the Three for Two spot on the tables at Waterstones, and the calls my agent had recently taken about the possibility of *Man Flu* being adapted for the screen.

Along with the nomination for this recent award. Which I think was being sponsored by a drinks company, newly into the arts racket. What was to be said about their motives? There were rumours about them, something to do with a video shoot that had ended badly, involving, as it apparently had done, a neo-Nazi pop group, and their lurid demise. Still, who cared about that? There was a thirty grand cheque in store for tonight's winner. Nobody was going to turn a prize like that down. And there was the prestige to consider.

So we made our way past the bouncer and on up the stairs, where we said hi to everyone on our table, Roger, Jeff and Alice, our long-suffering agent, editor and publicity person respectively.

'Michael,' said Alice, 'I thought we talked about this? Perhaps Lavender Bunny would be happier in the bar downstairs?'

'Would you like that, LB?'

'No Mike, I wouldn't.'

'Maybe he'd be happier in the Gents?'

'Alice, Lavender Bunny is giving you a hard stare.'

'Michael, I will pay, out of my own pocket, for Lavender Bunny to have as many cans of fizzy pop and shots on the bloody fruit machine as he likes until the speeches are over. I thought that's what we agreed?'

'But Alice, this is his night too.'

'You're still insisting on that, are you?'

'I can't not. Credit where credit's due.'

'Michael, how many more times? You wrote the book.

Not that fucking sock puppet.'

But Alice . . .'

'No Michael, I'm not going through this again!'

'What's the deal here?' said Roger.

'That thing . . . that fucking thing, is an inhuman monster. That's what the fucking deal is here Roger, all right?'

Alice had been a bit of a wild child, by all accounts, back in the day. But now she was a New Mum, fresh off maternity leave and commuting to London from somewhere in the green belt, where she was no doubt already the terror of the local pony club. We'd done some publicity together, LB, Alice and I, and it's fair to say we hadn't gelled as a team. Late night, at some literary festival, Alice had accused LB of being, and I quote 'a fucking monster. And a bad influence.'

'She knows me so little, Mike,' he'd sighed.

Anyway;

'Look Alice,' I said, 'It's not like we're going to win, or anything.'

'Phew,' blustered Alice, throwing back her copper-coloured curls, 'Good. I'm relieved to hear you say that. Honestly, *Man Flu* – what a lot of nonsense!'

'Alice,' said Jeff, sighing into his scotch, 'You're not supposed to say that in front of them.'

'I'll say what I want, Jeff. Thank you very much. I am a mother!'

' . . . ' said LB.

'What was that?'

'He said you're a mother, ah, something.'

'Oh god!' bellowed Alice, 'Why the fuck is this happening? I have to get home to my family!'

'I have to get home to your family first, Alice.'

'Shush, LB.'

Time to get a drink then.

We mingled for a while, taking in the crowd. The place

was unexpectedly packed. On the way to the bar, factions were clear. There was Kevin from Tyneside's table, there was the Scottish guy's table, there was the Welshman's table, and there was the Parson's table, bad vibes radiating from all of them.

'Mike?'

'Yes, LB?'

'I'd like to incinerate everyone in this room.'

'LB, they can hear you . . .'

'Well they're not really people, are they Mike?' said LB, already sounding heartbroken, 'I can't see Billie Piper, Vic Reeves or All Saints. Not even Burchill's here . . .'

'It'll all seem better after a large scotch.'

'That's your solution to everything, isn't it, Mike?'

'Well, yeah . . . but we've already established I'm going to hell when I die, unless I repent.'

'You should do that eventually, Mike. Better safe than sorry.'

'But not now?'

'No, Mike,' said LB, giving the other tables a hard stare, 'There are a few miles yet to travel, before we sleep.'

I don't know if you've ever been confronted by 'a face like thunder'. It's a commonplace, right, with no real meaning? That's what I thought, too. But storms were gathering around the Parsons table, like Tony's people would have happily taken a straight razor to the pair of us, as we drifted on by. I've said that Parsons had been negative about us on social media – that's true. What I've perhaps neglected to mention is that LB had given as good as he'd got, and then some.

For example, Parsons had said that *Man Flu* was 'derivative' and 'clearly an attempt, which will hopefully fail, to cash in on the works of greater writers, such as Nick Hornby, and myself.'

LB, in response, had said that Parsons should be

medically castrated. There had been a back and forth on Twitter. Not really a problem, as things go, but it's difficult, in a small place, to know what to say, when you're next to the guy in the drinks queue

'Tony,' I said.

'Michael. Lavender Bunny.'

'Parsons.'

'I saw you on Jonathan Ross the other week.'

'Great,' I said. 'Did you enjoy the show?'

'Well, I enjoyed Coldplay's performance.'

'Right. Do you like Coldplay?'

'No.'

'I bet you do really, Parsons,' said LB. 'They're like your books, aren't they? Boring material for depressed people in airports?'

'Fuck off, Lavender Bunny.'

'Mike, he's not to talk to me like that, is he?'

'D'you wanna make summing of it?'

'I'm considering it. You're saying, Tony, that Mike and I were worse than Coldplay?'

'That is exactly what I am saying.'

'Man, that's . . . I would never say that . . .'

'Glass him Mike,' said LB.

'You reckon you could take me?'

'No, I . . .'

'Yes Parsons! Mike does!'

'He doesn't really . . .'

'Any time, Michael . . .'

'Okay,' I said catching the barman's attention, and getting my round in before Tony's – this seemed important, 'A pair of large scotches, and for you, Tony?'

'Nothing for me, Michael. I'll be drinking champagne later. Shall I tell you what I don't like about you?

'He went on for a while, until,

'What, in a massage parlour?' LB said.

'You haven't been listening to a word I've been saying,

have you? Look at you. Both of you. You drugged-out losers.'

'You're the loser, Parsons.'

'No, I ain't,' Tony said. 'My novels have consistently delivered. They have been number one in the British sales charts, and translated into many languages.'

'So you've done an Archer? Well played, Parsons!'

Visibly, Tony was having trouble restraining himself. He was a novelist, wasn't he? Not a man of violence. But then I suppose he remembered about Norman Mailer, who used to get into it all the time at literary awards ceremonies.

'Anyway,' he snapped, 'It's nice to see you've brought your teddy bear along, Michael.'

'Who are you calling a teddy bear, Parsons?' said LB 'And who are you to accuse Mike of holding on to his childhood, like a nonce, when all you do is write about football?'

'That is *not* all I write about!'

'Tis'

'Right, I can see what's going on here. Winnie the Pooh is a middle class snob, and Christopher Robin, his sidekick, is shooting up?'

'Upper middle class snob, Parsons. And let's face it, Mike and I are household names. What are you?'

'I am a household name.'

'No, you're not.'

'Yes,' he hissed. 'I am. And off the sweat of my brow. Not for making a tit of myself on reality television. I ain't even read your novel.'

'That's good,' said LB, 'You wouldn't have understood it anyway.'

'What's that supposed to mean?'

'Well, school of hard knocks for you, wasn't it Parsons? University of life?'

'Shut up! Fuck you! What do you know about how real people live?'

'Enough.'

'Oh yeah?'

'I've burning them in Hell for centuries, Parsons.'

'Right. I've had enough of this. Let's take the discussion outside.'

Tony Parsons in some ways resembles Vladimir Putin. Physically, psychologically. He's a man of an age with a certain agenda (something to do with immortality?) and he doesn't care who knows it.

The tension was heavy in the alleyway, then. It was the strangest thing. It seemed like I was holding a beer in one hand, and Linsey Dawn McKenzie's number on speed-dial in the other. so all I could do was watch, as LB squared up to an angry Tony. A man's man versus a small bunny.

'I've got this, Mike.'

'I don't know, LB. Parsons doesn't drink, apparently, or read much, so what does he get up to when he isn't at his desk?'

'He goes to the gym?'

'He goes to the gym.'

'But Mike, he says everything he thinks about modern fiction is still valid?'

'Oh. Well, I suppose in that case . . .'

But while LB and I were discussing our strategy, Parsons, a seasoned street fighter, no doubt, blind-sided us. In a sucker move, he ducked, dived, then grabbed hold of LB and threw him onto the pavement. Where he gave him a stomping with, I was ashamed to note, the exact same brand of Chelsea boot I was wearing.

'I am the Daddy!' Tony was yelling, as, ambling out of the doorway (presumably, this kind of thing happened all the time at the Groucho – raging egos plus a lot of beer and coke) the bouncer intervened.

'Gents, sorry to interrupt, but the winner of the award is about to be announced?'

'Right,' said Tony, dusting himself off. 'Cigarette, or

should I say fag break over then, Lavender Bunny?'

'Parsons,' LB croaked, 'Fuck yourself.'

'Yeah. I get a lot of prizes. But I'm looking forward to this one in particular, Lavender Bunny. I want to send a message out to younger writers about what popular literature, about what communicating to your audience actually means.'

He kicked LB again, and then off he went.

'LB,' I said, blurred – was I coughing blood, coughing grit? – 'LB? You're indestructible, right?'

'I don't know Mike,' he replied, drifting, in a pool of cig butts, stale ale and leaves, looking up at the stars. 'Maybe not this time.'

'But LB, you're immortal?'

'Mike, I am, and I'm not. He . . . I think it's going to be difficult'

He seemed to fade in my arms, in that rain-drenched Soho alleyway. You can't kill ideas, not really, and you can't kill art. But if anyone was going to have a shot, who better than the author of *Man And Boy*?

'I heard that.' said Tony, running back over to give LB an extra shoeing, before he was restrained by the bouncer. 'You know nothing about what books ordinary people want to read . . . you fucking wanker . . .'

There was a silence out there by the bins, as Tony was escorted back inside.

'Are you all right there, mate?' said the bouncer

'Yeah . . .'

'You don't look all right.'

'No . . . everything seems quite distant.'

'Mike,' said LB 'It will be okay.'

'You don't seriously think that, do you?'

'I suppose not, no.'

Back in the club, walking through the tables, I had the

sense that Parsons, in our absence, may have been dripping poison into some of the other contestants' ears.

Kevin McManus, for example, had written a novel about growing up in Tyneside. The boats were in the harbour, rotting away, and all that. There were nay fish left on the dish. No cod, no haddock, nothing. The men of the family could no longer put food on the table, so every voyage was potentially their last. *Geordie Shore* meets *Jaws*, via *The Wasteland* – fine. Tam McPherson's' book, meanwhile, (you've got to love the 'Tam' – what a twat, and I can say that because he threw a chair at me later) was about an ex-mining community in Fife. If this stuff had been played for laughs I'd have been a fan. But these guys were serious. It was becoming increasingly clear that *Man Flu,* with it's relatively optimistic message, in the sense that the developers didn't win, *had no place* on this list. I'd assumed that everyone had written their books for cash and a movie deal, or counter-culture credibility, but apparently not. And I felt for them – whatever soul I'd had was long gone, but I could just about remember what it was like to want to make a difference to anything other than my bank account. On the other hand though, they had killed LB. So it was with mixed feelings and a heavy heart that I slumped back down with Jeff, Alice and Roger. LB limp in my hands.

'Christ,' said Roger.

'Is he all right?' said Alice, peering over the top of her Brick Lane, heavy-framed glasses, looking even more like a sweating red-faced bull than usual. 'Because it looks, to me, like Lavender Bunny has finally had his maker.'

'Yeah?'

'Yeah.'

'Alice, if we win this, I think I'm going to complain to Clarence about you. Clarence *and* Annabel.'

'You wouldn't dare . . . you can't fire me, Michael.'

'It was his dying wish that I'd try, Alice.'

'Roger?' Alice roared. 'Jeff?'

'He can get you into trouble, Alice'

'If he wins.'

It's an ask, I guess.'

'Indeed. Not so brave without our soldier to protect us now, are we, Michael?'

And really, I wasn't. It was painful to admit that even a stopped clock could be right twice a day. I hadn't minded beforehand, but now I desperately wanted to win this prize, as an homage to LB, yes, and also to show Parsons who was the king, and earn Alice a well-deserved bollocking from the company's owners. It wasn't going to happen, though, or so I thought. I was consumed by sadness, almost oblivious as the applause erupted, for Tony, I figured, or one of the regional authors – what was I going to do now? Who was going to write the next novel? How was I going to be able to buy all the cocaine I needed without LB?

But it's always darkest before the dawn. Keith Allen, I finally noticed, was on stage, as the master of ceremonies. He looked wired out of his mind, so some things, reassuringly, never change. and perhaps it was the energy of his celebrity that revitalised LB, when *Man Flu* was announced as the winner of that years Smirnoff prize for literature.

'Shit!' shouted Alice.

'You could have just muttered that, Alice,' I said.

'Mike,' said Jeff, 'One foot in front of the other. Aim yourself at the stage. It'll be okay. Though it might be best if you left LB here'

'I can't leave him behind, Jeff. This is his award as much as mine.'

'But Mike, he's dead. Parsons killed him.'

'No Jeff,' said a small voice, 'He didn't.'

It was a long walk through the crowd, past the Scottish

guy, past the writer from Tyneside, past the Parsons table, but by the time LB strode up to the lectern, he was like ten men, positively Churchillian. Grace in victory, it transpired, was not something he did. And as for the trend, fairly recent, for the artist to be diffident, self-deprecating and grateful for the opportunity to be read, or heard, or have hits on their website . . . that wasn't going to happen.

'Hello, small people,' he began, bedraggled, beaten-up, but defiant. 'I'd like to thank Mike for doing the typing, and nobody else. We won this because we are better than you. That is all. Bring on the Booker! Good night!'

Brevity is a virtue. In the spirit of this, the question was how we were going to get out of the building quickly enough.

Parsons didn't need the money, but the others, Kevin, Tam, the Welsh guy, could have done with it.

'Mike . . .'

'I know, I know . . . the atmosphere's ugly, we should leave?'

'I'm not frightened of these people, Mike.'

This as Kevin from Tyneside, who'd tried to push me into the gents facilities earlier, with, admittedly, some success, threw his pint at the lectern. Had he gone to the bathroom in the glass? Quite possibly. The liquid looked ominous. It was at this point Keith Allen got stuck in, as did the Scotsman, and the ceremony descended into an orgy of violence, like a Wild West bar fight, chairs flying everywhere. Well, thirty grand wasn't chump change. The Parsons table, I noticed, was heading fast for the exit, as if on the run from a marriage to Julie Burchill. Who was from Wales originally, I believe. Somewhere like that. Fair enough. Writers who aren't from London may have their plus points, but they can be aggressive.

'Well, they've got nothing to live for, have they, Mike?'

Regional literature at this stage made it clear what it thought about metropolitan elitists like LB and I.

'Mike,' said LB later, in the cab on the way to A&E; I had a busted nose for sure, and possibly also a couple of cracked ribs, there was blood everywhere, my shirt was like a Jackson Pollack improv, in dark red. 'I don't know about you, but I feel like we've arrived.'

'Yeah . . . I'm kind of struggling to move now, LB.'

'But Mike, we have won the award. There will be many more to follow.'

'Hopefully,' I said, as we stopped on Warren Street for cigs and beer, the guy on the till looking taken aback, 'Not too many more.'

And then the taxi rolled off, into fame, glory and so forth It costs, is all I'd say. This wasn't to be the last time LB and I wound up half-dead in the back of a taxi, after a literary awards ceremony. He said he was going to rearrange things so the world was more amenable, Dr Faustus style, and, in fairness, that's exactly what he did. There was the Whitbread, which we didn't win ('I'm sorry, Mike') and then there was the Booker, which, controversially, we were invited to judge – they were looking to expand the panel, to introduce a more populist element. Everyone (and it was pretty much everyone – Ian McEwan, Martin Amis, critics from the Observer books section – our new enemies, basically) who dissed LB was going to have to rethink their approach to the afterlife.

'I'll be seeing them again soon, Mike. Don't worry. I've made a few calls. Like if you'd ordered a pizza.'

'The flames are being stoked?'

'The flames are being stoked.'

'Excellent . . . but I grow weary, LB.'

'Not to say that, Mike.'

Walking into the Big Brother house, all those years ago, we'd started out with a bad reception. It was perhaps only germane if things ended the same way. If I have any regrets, sitting here with a loaded shotgun and a bottle of scotch, LB floating about above the table '(Don't do it,

Mike! We have years ahead of us! I'll have to find somebody else . . .') top of the list would be that we weren't up for the Nobel, and that consequently, LB never got to meet Bob Geldof, or the guy from U2, or the Pope, or the Dalai Lama. Annie Lennox, Tony Blair, Dave Lee Travis . . . Alan Sugar, Duncan from Dragon's Den . . . it was a longer list than I thought it would be. Although we did meet Alan Sugar; how could I have forgotten about that?

'Exactly, Mike. Let's be honest, is our work done?'

"But will our work ever be done? What is our work?"

'You know what our work is, Mike. And we have to keep on keeping on, don't we?'

'Well . . .'

'You get to act in life, Mike. What follows is characterised by its impotence. Charles Dickens, in *A Christmas Carol*, was not wrong.'

'The chained, lost souls?'

'Yeah.'

'All right,' I said, reluctantly putting the gun down, 'So what's next?'

'I'm glad you asked me that, Mike. Because I've been considering it for some time. I think if we . . . I don't know, bombed next year's Nobel ceremony, or something?'

'It would raise the temperature of the award, I guess . . . okay then, let's do that. Or at least, let's sit around talking about bombing the Nobel over a couple of bowls of crystal meth?'

'Mike,' said LB, 'That sounds ideal!'

11746980R00110

Printed in Great Britain
by Amazon.co.uk, Ltd.,
Marston Gate.